For Dawn Michelle Dorr Parr
A great friend and shining star on stage and off

One

He was going to kiss her. They wouldn't skirt around it with a wimpy hug or light peck on the cheek. The kiss would be full to the mouth and knee-buckling romantic. He leaned toward her. She stepped back. Her hands fluttered, but her eyes revealed her calm confidence. He grabbed her shoulders, pulling her to him. He paused for half a second before he began the long, passionate kiss. Her arms gripped his back, keeping him near.

"Whoa! Hold up a second, you two. Fire alarms are going to start ringing all over the building if you don't cool it. This isn't a soap opera—it's high school drama. Kisses have to be toned down. Don't forget, you're kissing for the audience, not your own pleasure.

"Felicia, hold off more. You're attracted to

Edmond, but you're suspicious he might be involved in the murder. I want to see both fear and longing on your face. Edmond, be more gentle. I want a romantic kiss, not a passionate kiss. There's a difference.

"Okay, let's try it again. Felicia, let me feel the romance. I want every girl in the audience who's never been kissed to live this kiss with you. All right? Let's take it from Edmond's entrance."

Edmond jogged off the stage before strolling back to begin his dialogue with Felicia. I had watched this scene so many times, I knew it by heart, but this time it was different. Even though Edmond wore jeans and a hoodie, I believed he was a gentleman standing in the library of a Victorian mansion. The romantic tension oozed from the stage in a thick, steady stream. He was going to kiss her again. I leaned forward as Edmond closed in on her. The sparks jumped between them when he took her in his arms. She didn't resist much before she succumbed. I held my breath.

She was good. Felicia let us girls who had

never been kissed live the kiss with her. If anyone could do it, Felicia could. Or, I should say, Amanda could. She's the one who drew us in. Felicia was her character's name. I didn't blink until Edmond released her.

"Okay, good. Much better." Mr. Elliot, the drama teacher, turned to whisper instructions to DeDe, the student director. Felicia and Edmond broke character as they laughed and gave each other high-fives.

I couldn't believe it. Amanda just received two of the most fabulous kisses imaginable—first hand, I might add—and now acted as if it were nothing. Acting. Maybe that was the problem. The kisses were part of the play. Enter stage left; cross to front center; kiss a beautiful guy.

The kisses weren't real. They didn't count. Still, I'd have taken them over my kissing experiences. Amanda was probably blasé about them because she had lived through enough real kisses to make these fake ones a joke to her. Some joke. Acting or not, Amanda would be kissed more times during the course of this play than I had been kissed in my entire life. With this last stage kiss, she had me beat, since I didn't count the two kisses I received from Jeff Harris when I was a freshman as real kisses.

Mr. Elliot's voice echoed through the auditorium. "I want to run through the first number in Act III before we call it quits for today."

DeDe clapped her hands. "That's the full chorus, Edmond and Miss Kline. Come on, places!"

I sprang to attention. Mrs. Fleming, the conductor, lifted her baton and, with a flick of her wrist, brought the pit orchestra to life. The pile of red hair she wore high on her head bounced in time to the snappy dance number we sent forth from the deep, dark recesses of the pit. Edmond boomed out the song with his strong, low voice, while members of the chorus whirled and wailed behind him.

My mouth settled into a serious line as I concentrated on the music. I didn't have to worry about lyrics or choreography, since I didn't have a leading role or even a part in the chorus.

4

I spent the long hours of rehearsal sitting on a hard chair at the bottom of a black hole. I was a member of the pit orchestra—first chair cellist, to be specific.

Actually, the pit wasn't all that deep and dark. It occupied the space between the front row of seats and the edge of the stage. A waist-high, portable black wall encircled it, pretending to make it a secluded area.

Despite the long, boring rehearsals, I enjoyed playing with the orchestra. Being a member of a group that produced amazing sounds and intricate melodies had always been an almost out-of-body experience for me. And, in all honesty, I played the cello better than anyone in our school. The cello was my passion. The sounds I coaxed from my instrument were dark and mysterious. Or they could be luscious and soothing, like sinking your teeth into a thick piece of fudge.

My eyes stayed focused on the happenings in the pit, the music on the stand in front of me and the directions from Mrs. Fleming, instead of darting to the action on stage. The orchestra had practiced with the cast every day after school for two weeks, and I'd seen the play more times than I cared to remember. My job now was to make the audience forget the orchestra existed by creating music that flowed seamlessly with the action of the play. It wouldn't be hard. The only lights in the pit were small music stand lamps. They were so dim we could barely read our sheet music. We dressed in black for performances. We were the invisible cast members.

"Hey, Brittany, can you give me a lift home after rehearsal?"

I glanced sideways to see Amanda lean over the pit barrier. She wore her floor-length, lace-covered, kissing-scene gown. She had started rehearsing in her costumes sooner than the rest of the cast. She called it "getting into the role." Whatever.

She wasn't in the number being rehearsed and had time to kill. I guess she decided to spend it trying to make me botch my part. Amanda, Miss Star-of-the-Play, had been my best friend since first grade.

My eyes darted back to my music sheet. "Yes," I hissed.

Mrs. Fleming's head snapped towards me. She was so small that the audience would have no problem seeing over her, despite the fact that she stood on a podium. Still, her piercing eyes and firm frown demanded instant and total obedience. Amanda took two steps away from the pit. After about five seconds, she came back and leaned close to whisper in my ear, which she could reach since I sat next to the pit barrier at the conductor's right.

"What did you think of that kiss?"

I shrugged one shoulder and tried to ignore her.

"He must have taken a swig of mouthwash right before we did the scene. I swear I tasted spearmint."

My next note came out as a screech.

"Amanda, do you mind?" I said with a crusty glare. "I'm trying to rehearse."

"Brittany!" Mrs. Fleming's tone meant business.

7

Amanda smiled before she covered her mouth with her hands and backed away. "Sorry. I do need a ride home though, okay?"

I nodded and turned back to my music. Where were we? My eyes wandered to the stage. Edmond, flanked by four chambermaids and backed up by half a dozen butlers, sang about the pleasures and perils of love and wealth. I nodded my head to the rhythm. He had a nice voice. He was pretty cute too. Why did Amanda get all the luck?

"We're at H," Marissa, the second chair cellist, whispered to me. Her dark hair and skin made her almost impossible to see in the dim pit. If I didn't look straight at her, she appeared to be a headless, armless white t-shirt playing a cello.

"Thanks," I said, scanning the music for the marker. The instant my eyes landed on it, I jumped back into the song.

:(♥): :(♥): :(♥):

In the orchestra room, after rehearsal, I snapped my case shut. I ran my fingers over the tiny bumps that covered it and debated whether

I should take my cello home or not. I could use the practice. The score for the play had a couple of tricky passages.

My cello was such a pain to lug home and back.

The thought of sitting in my room lost in rich sounds and gentle melodies sounded really good to me.

I had a pile of homework to plow through.

I hadn't practiced at home in three days.

Amanda was riding home with me.

That decided it. I couldn't fit both her and my cello in my car at the same time. My cello didn't fit in the trunk. The only way to squeeze it in was to lower the passenger seat to its full reclining position and lay the cello on it like a sleeping commuter. Oh well. I could take it home tomorrow and have the whole weekend to practice.

I stowed my instrument in its designated cupboard and headed back to the auditorium to search for Amanda. Cast and crew members gathered in clusters across the stage and throughout the rows of velvet lined seats. She had to be among them somewhere. I sat down on one of the chairs to wait, hoping she'd appear before long.

Minutes ticked away. Most of the groups broke up, as kids grabbed backpacks off chairs and traipsed up the aisles to the exit doors. Where was Amanda? Was she having a meeting backstage with Mr. Elliot or something?

The seat next to mine bounced as Robert, the butler—I didn't know his real name—sat down.

"You're Brittany, right?" he asked.

I nodded. My heart shifted into high gear, and my tongue felt as if a glob of glue had been spread across it. Why did this happen every time a boy came within two feet of me? Especially a cute boy. Amanda stayed calm and in perfect control around guys.

"The play's turning out okay, don't you think?" asked Robert. "I think we'll be ready to open next week."

"Yeah. Yes. We'll be ready," I said through the glue.

"I almost didn't try out for it," he said, not

seeming to notice my tangled tongue. "I mean, who wants to be in a play the school's drama teacher wrote? When I found out it was a musical-murder-mystery-romance, I almost ran out of auditions so fast the track coach wouldn't have been able to catch me."

I laughed. "You know, I thought the same thing. When I learned Mrs. Fleming composed the songs, I didn't want anything to do with this production." Hey, I spoke rationally! Who washed the glue out of my mouth?

"We can't hide the fact that this play is corny, but I think we're going to pull it off."

"The cast is doing great," I said. "The way everyone sings those songs is amazing. It turned out Mrs. Fleming is a pretty good composer. I heard she'd been writing songs for years as a hobby. She made a ton of changes during the first two weeks of orchestra rehearsals, but the songs turned out okay. Don't you think?"

"I think they're great," Robert said with a smile. He was nice looking, especially when he smiled. I couldn't believe I sat there chatting with him like an old buddy. I could get used to this. I could stand to be around Robert more. A lot more. I wondered what his real name was. If I asked, would he be offended I didn't know?

"But," Robert said, "the real credit for pulling off this play has to go to Amanda."

Screeeeeeeeeech. The brakes on my thumping heart kicked in, but not fast enough to keep it from plunging off a cliff and somersaulting to a fiery explosion at the bottom of a canyon. I should have paid attention to the warning signs.

Robert didn't notice my smile weaken as he sang the praises of Amanda, a tune I was very familiar with.

"Her voice is unbelievable. She can act, too. And the way she looks—wow. You're friends with her, right?"

I nodded, my toothy, fake grin frozen in place.

Robert slid his arm onto the back of my chair and leaned toward my ear as if he were going to tell me a secret. "Is there any way you could—you know—put in a good word for me?"

R-r-r-rip. I pried the clownish, I'm-happy-everything's-okay smile off my face as I turned my head from him. I stared at the stage while I spoke with a voice as flat and lifeless as my soul. "Amanda knows you better than I do. I'll bet she even knows your name."

"I know she knows who I am, but she doesn't really *know* me. I thought if the two of us pretended to be friends, we could hang out together—with Amanda. You know, we could get to know each other on a casual level. Once we're friends, it'll be easy to ask her out. What do you say?"

I rolled my eyes. "Amanda has a boyfriend. Everyone in school knows that."

"They broke up today," Robert said, twitching his eyebrows and smiling like a rat who stole cheese from a trap without getting caught.

"Really." I wasn't surprised, just disappointed he shot down my excuse so easily. Amanda had been going with Jeremy for three weeks, a record for her. I thought she'd finally settled down.

I leaned forward, ready to rise from my seat, while I scanned the auditorium. Where was

Amanda anyway?

"Here's what I thought we'd do," said Robert, oblivious to my discomfort. "Amanda and Kyle just left for the golden arches. You and I will head over there right now. It'd be natural for us to share a booth with them. We'll have to hurry though."

My mind stuck on his first comment. "Amanda left with who?"

"Kyle. You know, Edmond from the play."

"Oh, Edmond." I hadn't known his real name because Mr. Elliot called everyone by their stage names during rehearsals, but that wasn't the point. Amanda left without telling me. How could she? I'd waited for her. Hadn't she asked me to give her a ride home? I had a lot to do that night, and I didn't enjoy being stood up by my supposed friend. She blew me off without a second thought to go on a date with her leading man.

I stood up, grabbed my backpack and started down the row of seats, in the opposite direction of Robert.

"Hey, Whitney, where are you going?" Robert called after me. "I thought we had a date."

14

"I'm busy," I said over my shoulder.

"Maybe some other time. How about tomorrow after rehearsal?"

I reached the end of the row. "Yeah, sure," I muttered before sprinting up the aisle.

"Great!" I heard him exclaim as I pushed through the swinging doors into the foyer of the school. Had he mistaken my sarcasm for enthusiasm? What an idiot! I slammed through the glass exterior doors and ran to the parking lot. My fingers shook as I unlocked my car door, but I didn't crumble until I sat safely inside and had driven a few blocks away from the school.

Why had I let that stupid butler talk to me the way he did without telling him what I thought? I didn't even correct him when he called me Whitney. Goes to show how much he cared about me. I was invisible to him in any way other than as a road leading straight to Amanda. I'd have to add another item to my list of dating rules.

Brittany's Rules for Dating:
1. I will never date anyone Amanda dated.

This limited my choices right off the bat. At the rate Amanda went through guys, not many remained in our high school to choose from. The chance to date post-Amanda guys presented itself to me often. Heartbroken cast-offs turned to me as a familiar face that reminded them of the brief moments they shared with her. I provided a shoulder to cry on and, they hoped, a link back to the woman they loved. I made the mistake of going out with an Amanda-ex once. After two hours of listening to him whine, cry and plead with me to talk to her about him, I vowed I'd never do it again.

2. *I will never date anyone who wishes he were dating Amanda.*

Almost any guy who didn't fit into the first category fit into this one. I refused to be someone's second choice. Being the I-can't-have-what-I-want-so-I'll-settle-for-you girl was not my idea of romance.

3. I will never kiss a guy who Amanda kissed.

Who wants their kissing ability compared to a pro?

And my new category:

4. I will never date a guy who uses me to get to Amanda.

These guys probably fit under rule number two, but it made me feel better to create a special category for that jerk, Robert.

I glanced at my white-knuckled hands strangling the steering wheel and loosened my grip. Pumping my fingers for a few seconds, I brought back the blood flow while steering with my palms.

Why did I let comments from guys like Robert get to me? I should've been used to them. Amanda was the star. I was a supporting member of the orchestra. Amanda shined on stage where all adored her. I sat invisible in the pit.

Two

As I tried to make sense of the Russian Revolution of 1905, the phone rang. I didn't budge from my seat at the kitchen table. I had two younger sisters. The phone would get answered.

Before the second ring died away, Brooke and Brianna raced around the corner into the kitchen, squealing as they fought over the right to answer the telephone. Yes, my parents decided it would be cute to give their children names that started with the same sound. If we girls had been boys, I'm sure our names would be Brian, Bradley and Bruce. My parents loved that 'Brrrrr' sound. Maybe they secretly wished their kids lived in Antarctica.

Brianna, being younger and more wiry, wrestled the phone from Brooke's grasp and blurted a giggly "Hello" into the mouthpiece. She listened for a few seconds before responding, "Yeah, she's right here, doing her homework without being told, as usual." Brianna listened for a few seconds before she grinned and gushed into the phone. "No, I'm only twelve. You know we're not allowed to date 'til we're sixteen." Brianna listened and giggled some more before she said good-bye and handed the phone to me. She beamed at Brooke. "Amanda says I should start thinking up good let-down lines for guys who ask me out before I turn sixteen. She says there's going to be lots of them."

"Only if the guys at your middle school are blind," said Brooke. With a flip of her hair, she stalked out of the kitchen.

Covering the phone with my palm, I called after Brooke. "Amanda would've said the same thing to you if you had answered." It was true. Amanda dished out compliments by the gallon. It was one of her methods of endearing herself to others. Hate to admit it, but it worked. Even on me, sometimes. Who didn't like to be complimented?

Brianna stood on the other side of the table, re-waiting to eavesdrop on my conversation.

"Don't you have something better to do?" I asked.

Shaking her head, she took a seat.

I sighed and placed the phone to my ear. "Hello."

"Hey! You'll never believe what happened after rehearsal today," Amanda said.

"What." I turned a page in my book, debating whether I could study and listen to the latest romantic encounter of Amanda Parker at the same time. I wouldn't hear anything I hadn't heard at least a dozen times before.

"Most of the leads went out to get some food," said Amanda. "We were starving after all that dancing and singing. We were sitting in the booth, talking—actually we were griping about what a psycho DeDe's turning out to be. I mean, some of the things she tells me to do make me wonder if she wants me to look like a total fool. When I question her she gets all huffy and stalks off with that little clipboard of hers. She acts like she's the goddess of student directors or something, and expects us to bow down and worship her." Amanda laughed. "We came up with this great name for her, DeDe the Demented Director of Doom."

"Amanda," I said, "did you call just to whine about DeDe? Because, if that's all you want to tell me, I can't take the time to listen. I have lots of homework to do. Maybe I would've had time to talk if I hadn't wasted an hour after rehearsal sitting in the auditorium waiting to give you a ride home."

Amanda paused. "I'm such an idiot. I totally forgot I asked you for a ride! You didn't really wait a whole hour, did you?"

"I guess it was more like ten minutes."

"Good." Subject closed for her. She kept going, "well, anyway, the reason I'm calling is to tell you someone has a crush on you."

"A-man-da." I slumped down, resting my forehead on the table. What I wanted to do was pound my head against the table. This announcement from her was not unusual. She regularly presented me with news of a possible romance in my near future. She did it partly because she felt guilty about the millions of guys who chased after her, while none were interested in me. But, mostly she did it because she cared about me and wanted to see me living happily ever after with a great guy. Nothing ever came of it, and it was really starting to drive me nuts. I needed to add another category to my list.

> 5. *I will never date a guy Amanda has chosen for me.*

Any guy she convinced to date me would only do it to increase his standing with her.

"I have to go, Amanda."

"Don't you want to know who he is?"

"Not really."

She ignored me. "See if you can guess. He's really cute. He has dark hair and green eyes. And he's super nice."

I snorted. "That narrows it down."

"Figure it out. I said I went out with the leads

after rehearsal, so. . . ."

"Please don't tell me it's Inspector Tisdale."

"You mean Russell Broberg? Nope—at least not that I know of."

"Well, I'm sure it's not the devious Miss Kline," I said, giving Brianna a wink across the table. She muffled her giggle with her palm.

"You're not even trying," said Amanda.

"Give me a better hint, but make it quick."

"Okay, okay. Let me see. Wait, I've got it." She cleared her throat and spoke in a deep, gravelly voice. "Felicia, I swear by my love for you, I had nothing to do with your uncle's murder."

"Edmond?" I gasped.

"Yes! Kyle."

"Oh yeah, Kyle."

"Yep, yep. You two will be great together."

I tapped my pencil eraser on the table. "Don't be silly, Amanda. We don't even know each other. You're the one he went out with today."

"We didn't go on a date. We were with five other people."

"He has to have a girlfriend, then. Guys that

hot always have a girlfriend."

"Something he said today made me think he used to go out with DeDe, but I know he's not with her now. He slammed her almost as much as I did. He's the one who came up with the demented part of DeDe the Demented Director of Doom."

"You like saying that, don't you," I said. "Anyway, what in the world, besides your very wild imagination, makes you think Edmond has a crush on me?"

"He said so."

"Right. He leaned across the table, ripped off a bite of french fry, looked you passionately in the eye and said, 'Darling, I'm madly in love with your friend. What was her name again?'"

"Actually, you're partly right. After rehearsal, when you were lugging your cello out of the pit, he asked me if I knew you."

I waited a few seconds for Amanda to continue. She didn't.

"That's it?" I asked.

"What more do you need? He wanted to

know who you were."

"And you take that to mean he has a crush on me."

"What else could it mean?"

"Hmmm, I can think of at least fifty things. One. I need to know who that girl is so I can ask her where she bought her shoes. They would look great on my girlfriend. Two. I need to know who that girl is so I can ask her for cello lessons. Three. I need to know who that girl is so I can ask her who cut her hair and avoid that stylist. Four. I need to know who that girl is so I can. . . ."

"Okay, okay. I admit there might be a slight possibility he meant something else, but I paid extra attention to everything he said this afternoon. Not once did he say anything about any other girl. He didn't mention you specifically either, but my instincts say he's interested in dating you. You know how reliable my instincts are."

Yeah. As reliable as the sun setting in the north. Amanda wasn't one to be talked out of her beliefs though, so I decided not to try.

"That's great, Amanda. I'll see you tomorrow."

"You don't believe me, but I don't care. I think he likes you, whether he knows it yet or not. Here's what we'll do. Tomorrow, during rehearsal sometime, I'll mention what a great job the pit orchestra is doing, one member of the orchestra in particular. I'll even put in a few words about how romantic the cello is and how passionate cellists are."

"You're crazy, Amanda. And if you so much as glance in my direction when you're around him, I'll steal your make-up, and you'll have to go to school with a blank face. You know perfectly well Edmond has no interest in me."

"Kyle."

I growled. "You know perfectly well *Kyle* has no interest in me. Any guy who knows the two of us always thinks of you as a potential date. Never me."

"Brittany. . . ."

"It's okay. It's not your fault. Some girls are born male-magnets, some aren't. There's not a whole lot we can do about it."

"But there is, Brittany. There's tons we can do about it."

"Oh, no," I said, shaking my head and waving my hands, even though Amanda couldn't see me. "No more make-overs or new hairstyles. We've done all that, and nothing changed. I'm not going to slave over a hot curling iron to impress a bunch of guys. If they don't like the way I look, that's their problem."

"You talk like you have thick glasses, braces, greasy hair and a face full of zits. Do you ever look in the mirror? You're gorgeous, Brittany. All you need to do is start believing it. Oops. I'm getting another call."

"It's Edmond. He's calling to ask you to do some extra rehearsing on that kissing scene."

"His name is Kyle, Brittany. And he doesn't need any practice, believe me. Maybe you'll find out for yourself soon. Talk to you tomorrow."

Amanda clicked off before I said good-bye. I shook my head and hung up the phone. As I sat back down, I noticed Brianna's eyes following me.

"Do you think I'll be a male-magnet when I'm older?" she asked.

"I don't know, Bree."

"I'd like to have lots of boyfriends like Amanda. Should I dye my hair dark and get a perm so I'll look more like her?"

"Absolutely not."

"Then what will make me a male-magnet?"

"I don't know. It's not any one thing. Looks aren't all of it, although they are a big part." I reached across the table and ruffled her hair. "I wouldn't worry too much about it if I were you. Being a male-magnet isn't necessarily a good thing."

"Why not? Wouldn't it be more fun to go on dates every weekend instead of. . . ."

"Instead of sitting home with your little sisters?"

She gave me a sheepish smile. "You don't sit home *every* weekend."

"I do enough of them. Listen, Bree, there's more to life than dating. A lot more. Most male-magnets don't realize that."

"Does Amanda?"

"Sure. I think. I mean, she thinks about guys more than she should, but she thinks about other things, too. She spends a lot of time on her acting and singing. You should see her in this play. She's good, really good. Decide what you like to do and work hard doing it. Boys will come when they come."

"You promise?"

I nodded, hoping I wasn't lying. I was still waiting for them to come myself. I stood up. "I'm going to study in my room."

"Brittany?" Brianna held me with her voice. "You told Amanda guys don't like the way you look. Is that true?"

I stood, paralyzed by the words coming from my sister, who looked almost the same as I had five years earlier.

"No, it's not true. Don't you ever goof around with your friends, saying things you don't mean?"

She grinned and nodded.

I smiled back before I gathered my books and headed up the stairs to the privacy of my bedroom. After making sure the door was shut tight behind me, I dumped my stuff on the bed.

Despite what I said to Amanda and Brianna, homework was the last thing on my mind. I slid onto the stool in front of the glass-and-chrome vanity, which held my small assortment of make-up and hair styling tools. My fingers rose to my face as I gazed into the mirror.

Hair. Sort of blah brown. A few nice high-lights lingered as a whisper of a memory of the summer sun. I released the clip at the back of my head and watched the lifeless strands tumble to my shoulders. I hadn't paid much attention to my hair lately. A few extra strokes with the brush and a little styling gel would make a difference.

Eyes. A pleasant light blue. Often described as my best feature. They were nice, I guess.

Nose. Average. At least it wasn't big or bumpy.

Lips. Ordinary. Kissable? Who knew.

Complexion. Not bad. Skin tended to break out every once in a while—one particular week each month. Go figure.

Cheeks, chin, forehead. I drew a blank. How did you rank a cheek? What made one forehead beautiful and another repulsive? You got me.

Overall. That was tough. I'd lived with my face my whole life. I was hardly the impartial judge I needed. I couldn't blindly believe Amanda's statement that I was gorgeous, either. What did someone seeing me for the first time think about my looks?

I closed my eyes for several seconds, pasted a toothy grin on my face and opened my eyes.

"Hi, I'm Brittany," I said to my reflection. Nah, too fake.

I fluffed my hair with my fingers, tilted my head and winked. Barf. Who was I kidding?

Okay, so I wasn't super-model material. I wasn't a Queen of the Nerds contender either. What about my comments to Brianna? Had I lied? Did guys like the way I looked or not? The evidence pointed in the direction of 'not.' Except, I knew I looked better than lots of girls who had boyfriends. Something besides my appearance was keeping guys at arms' length. I'd have to figure out what it was. I would, too. Sometime.

31

Three

Dress rehearsal progressed fairly smoothly. A cast member missed a line or cue here and there. Two of the party guests collided as they danced across the stage. One piece of scenery wobbled precariously, while another failed to appear at all. No one worried much about the flubs. Everything would pull together the next day for the first performance, a matinee for local elementary school students.

That show was more of a second dress rehearsal. What did kids know or care about theater? They'd be happy no matter what we did onstage if it got them out of a few hours of classwork. The show for the students at our school, during the last two class hours Thursday afternoon, would be a small step up from the elementary kids. Our first performance for adults would take place Thursday night, followed by evening shows on Friday and Saturday.

The end of the play drew near. The kissing scene was up next, followed by the finale. This was the only play I'd heard of where the final scene contained the uncovering of a murderer, the announcement of an engagement and the performance of an extravagant song and dance number. If you ignored how silly it was, it was actually kind of good.

Felicia retreated to the library to escape the anxiety of the party Inspector Tisdale organized to flush out the murderer. Edmond followed to express his love for her. Since he was one of the prime suspects, Felicia hesitated to admit she returned his affections. Fear and romance covered the stage like dense London fog.

I didn't watch Amanda and Kyle. I listened for my cues, watched Mrs. Fleming's baton and provided intense musical background for the scene. Amanda hadn't mentioned my blooming romance with Kyle, as she put it, since the phone call last Thursday night. She probably forgot about it since she was on to a new romance her-self. She went out with Jared, the chief stagehand person—or whatever his title was—after rehears-al yesterday. From what I heard on the phone last night, she'd found true love at last. At least for this week.

I was relieved Amanda forgot about Kyle. Knowing her, if she remembered, she would have spent every spare second backstage feeding him juicy tidbits about me, when, in reality, he didn't hunger after me at all.

The scene ended, fear yielding to love once more, and the curtains closed to allow the stage crew to set up for the finale. Next to me, Marissa giggled. Everyone in the pit giggled.

"What'd I miss?" I whispered over the inter-lude music.

"Didn't you see what she did?"

"Who? Amanda?"

Marissa nodded. "She came out wearing the most ghastly shade of fuchsia lipstick. Kyle still had to kiss her, so he was covered with it before the scene ended. Mr. Elliot is going to kill her, but it was hilarious."

Leave it to Amanda.

She must have scrubbed her face fuchsia-free in the seconds between scenes. She came out wearing a nice stage red for the finale. It went off without a hitch, and the curtains closed.

Mr. Elliot and DeDe, the only audience members, clapped three times. DeDe leaned over to talk to Mr. Elliot. She wore her hair in a tight ponytail. Oval, wire rimmed glasses perched on her nose. She never wore the glasses away from rehearsals, and her hair hung loose whenever I saw her in the halls. I guess she wanted to look artsy or domineering around the cast and crew. Truth was, the look worked. I wouldn't want to meet her in a dark hallway.

She took her job as student director very seriously. DeDe the Demented Director of Doom. She probably told Mr. Elliot to crack down hard on Amanda, that if she went unpunished, her pranks would spoil the play. Whatever she said didn't work.

Mr. Elliot, having directed high school theater for over twenty years, understood the need for teenagers to release some of their pre-opening jitters. When he called the cast onstage for some final instructions, the only remark he made about Amanda's joke was, "We are serious performers. Let's not give our audience any reason to believe we are clowns."

A wide-eyed Amanda nodded her head, as if Mr. Elliot couldn't have been more right. After he ended rehearsal with a few words of encouragement and strict counsel for everyone to get a good night's sleep, Amanda turned to the cast members around her and grinned. Mr. Elliot called Jared forward from the cluster of stage crew members, and the two of them, along with DeDe, huddled over a clipboard of notes as they strolled up the aisle and disappeared into the control booth. The second the door clunked shut, Amanda pulled a tube of lipstick from her pocket and slathered a thick layer on her lips.

"Who's next?" she asked, turning to the rest of the cast.

"Me!" all the guys yelled. One of them

snatched the lipstick from her and plastered it on himself. He passed it off to another guy and raced to catch a nearby parlor maid. Soon the entire cast and crew wore bright pink lips and numerous lip-marks on their cheeks.

Mrs. Fleming chuckled as she gathered her music and baton. "You kids have better ways of dealing with stress than most grown-ups." She climbed out of the pit and headed for the orchestra room. I saw a few sly glances and 'why-not' shrugs from the other orchestra members. They set down their instruments and scrambled up to the stage.

I found myself alone in the pit. As I debated whether to join the lipstick craze or slink back to the orchestra room, I felt a tap on my shoulder. A beaming Amanda, face covered with lip-marks, leaned over the barrier.

"I never dreamed it would get this wild."

"Didn't you, now," I said with a scolding smile. I stood up.

Before Amanda answered, a guy from the chorus leaped down from the stage and bounced over to us. Amanda and I stood close enough for him to grab one of us in each arm and pull us in for a tight three-way hug. Without a word, he released us and jumped back onto the stage to grab other unsuspecting females.

I noticed a fresh lip-mark on Amanda's face. My hand rose to my cheek. Had he planted one on me too? Amanda must have seen the question in my eyes. She shook her head, almost imperceptibly, in reply.

No. Of course not. No guy wanted to kiss me, even as part of a game.

The clunk of a door made Amanda turn. "It's Jared. His face is way too clean." She pulled a fresh tube of lipstick from her pocket, covered her lips and raced up the aisle to greet him. Jared stood in front of the control room door, gaping at the scene onstage. Anger crinkled the corners of his tight-set mouth.

Amanda grabbed his arm and smooshed her lips into his cheek. The kiss was enough to erase his tension. He allowed her to pull him down the aisle to join the others onstage.

The control room door clunked again. DeDe looked angrier than Jared had. Her eyes narrowed into slits as they scanned the stage. She lowered her gaze to the pit and rested her eyes on me. What? I hadn't done anything wrong. In case she hadn't noticed, the only lipstick-free face in the room belonged to me.

DeDe marched toward the stage, clipboard in hand. Everyone with pink lips was about to get chewed out. She stomped up the stairs and disappeared in the crowd. A moment later I saw her—lips covered, glasses gone—jump on Edmond, piggyback style. He looked more surprised than he does when Miss Kline walks into his bedroom in the play. DeDe stretched her neck and dotted his cheek with lip-marks. Maybe she had another side to her besides the Demented Director of Doom. Edmond lifted one corner of his mouth and spun in slow circles while she clung to his neck. So much for his breakup with her and new interest in me.

I couldn't stand alone in the pit any longer. Holding my cello and bow in one hand, I picked up my music folder by the corner with the other. A piece of paper slipped to the ground. It was small—too small to be sheet music. I set down my music folder, and reached through the jumble of chairs and music stands to snatch up the paper. It was a note. I almost dropped my cello as I read the stinging words.

Why are you friends with her?
What's so great about Amanda Parker anyway?
Why can't someone else have a chance every once in a while? I hope she croaks before the play closes—along with anyone stupid enough to be friends with her.

I glanced around the auditorium. Who wrote this? And why? Why would someone put a note like this in my music folder? Were they just venting steam?

It was easy to become jealous of Amanda. I'd done it many times myself. In fact, I'd asked myself those same questions a thousand times. I hadn't written the note in my sleep, had I? When I woke from those jealous dreams, I always realized it wasn't fair to be angry with Amanda because she had something I didn't.

Over the years, we'd spent more hours giggling together than we'd spent in school. I couldn't count how many sleepless sleepovers we'd shared. I wasn't petty enough to give up our friendship over something as stupid as jealousy. Besides, we still had tons of fun together—although that time seemed to get shorter and shorter with each new boyfriend.

I crumpled the note in my hand. Oh well. If someone wanted to release their anger towards Amanda by writing me anonymous little notes, I couldn't see the harm in it. I certainly wasn't going to waste any time worrying about it.

I shoved the note into the pocket of my blue jeans. I didn't have to wear black until the real performance. I picked up my music folder, once again, and climbed the set of stairs to the stage. I took a deep breath, steeling myself for the treacherous journey past props, scenery and several dozen lipstick crazy teenagers. I only half-listened to the voices in the crowd as I walked.

"Check her out."

"We can't let her leave like that."

"Hand me the lipstick."

Before I knew what was happening, I found myself surrounded by the guys from the pit orchestra, and a few from the cast and crew.

"I'll take that for you," said L.J., the percussionist, as he pulled away my cello, bow and music folder.

Screaming and laughing, I tried to shield my face. No luck. Two guys held down my arms while they, and everyone else around, attacked. My face must have been a solid sheet of fuchsia before they let me go.

"Your instrument, Madame," said L.J. after the others retreated. I took my cello and bow and reached for my music folder. L.J. snatched up my hand, probably the only spot of unmarked skin he could find, and gave it a sticky, pink kiss. He shoved the folder into my arms, bowed deeply and dashed away to chase Marissa.

I stood in a daze for a moment. I couldn't stop the smile from growing on my face.

The madness on the stage subsided as the cast and crew drifted away. Most of the members of the orchestra climbed back into the pit to grab their instruments. I noticed Amanda smile at Uncle Conrad when he returned her tube of lipstick. As she shoved it in her pocket, her eyebrows crinkled together.

Amanda stood alone among the dozen or so stragglers as she pulled a slip of paper from her pocket. My heart skipped a beat. Could it be? Amanda frowned as she scanned the note. She glanced over her shoulder before she dropped her eyes to study it once more. From the look on her face, I knew the tone, if not the exact content. Sending me a vicious note about Amanda was one thing; I could ignore it easily enough. Sending one to Amanda was another.

I walked toward her, but before I made it halfway across the stage, Jared appeared. He claimed her by draping an arm around her shoulders. She shoved the note into her pocket and beamed up at him. I wasn't fooled. Her eyes betrayed her uneasiness. The note had gotten to her.

I couldn't help her at the moment. I'd have to call later to offer my support and comfort. Jared led her towards the back of the stage. As they took their first step past the scenery into the blackness of the curtain jungle beyond, Amanda hesitated. She pulled away from him, saying a few words. He shrugged. She turned. Her eyes darted in a frantic search around the stage until they landed on me.

"Brittany! Thank heavens you're still here." Amanda pranced across the stage with Jared ambling up behind her. "We're going to Malley's for shakes. Come with us."

I gave her a one-sided smile. "Thanks, but I've got to get home." I knew Amanda felt uneasy at the moment and needed me as her security blanket. I'd often been recruited as a crutch for her to lean on in new or uncertain situations. The worst was the time last summer when she dragged me to watch a guy she liked compete in a track meet. It wasn't bad—until his events ended. He sat next to Amanda on the bleachers and gave me sideways glares every few minutes, as if he had been there first and I was an intruder.

After a while, he went to buy soft drinks. He returned with one for him and one for Amanda. It was as if he said to me, "As far as I'm concerned, you're not even here." I was the ugly toad sitting next to the prince and princess as they chatted over cold drinks.

Amanda was sensitive enough to offer me a sip of her drink at one point. I told her I wasn't thirsty. I should have left right then, but—silly me—I thought Amanda needed a ride home. Of course, I found myself alone after the meet, while Amanda snuggled up to her new boyfriend in his car. He only lasted three days. I shouted for joy when she dumped that insensitive jerk. Anyway, as you might suppose, I wasn't anxious to repeat the experience any time in the near or distant future.

"Please come, Brittany. It will be fun."

I pulled her aside and lowered my voice. "You don't really want me to come. The note upset you, and you're not thinking straight."

"What note?" Amanda asked, flipping her hair over her shoulder.

"I got one too."

"You did?" A spark of hope returned to her eyes.

"Call me when you get home. We'll talk about it then. Okay?"

"I want you to come with us." She pressed her lips together.

"Forget it. I'm not in the mood to be a third wheel."

"You won't be. Lots of the cast and crew will be there. You want her to come with us, don't you, Jared?"

Talk about putting a guy on the spot. Of course he didn't want me to come with them. He also didn't want to displease Amanda. He shrugged his shoulders.

"Whatever."

"I have to change out of my costume and

wash off this lipstick. Go put your stuff away and meet us back here in ten minutes."

"Amanda..."

"Ten minutes."

Four

With my face scrubbed fuchsia-free, my cello stored in the orchestra room and my backpack, heavy with that evening's homework, slung over my shoulder, I pulled open the door to the backstage area. I didn't care how much Amanda pleaded or how firmly she demanded: I wasn't going to Malley's. I just had to figure how to tell her. Surely Jared would be on my side.

Darkness covered the stage. The hollow silence in the auditorium told me everyone had gone home. Once Amanda tucked the lipstick away, I guess no one saw any reason to stick around.

A pair of giggles cut through the stillness. It had to be Amanda and Jared. It didn't take her long to get over her uneasiness with him. Would I make her angrier by backing out of the trip to

Malley's, or by barging in on her private time with her boyfriend in the dark auditorium?

I shuffled past props and scenery, feeling my way through the black curtains until I broke through onto the open stage. Two figures huddled near the pit, next to my chair. The lamp on my music stand provided the only light. As I suspected, Amanda made up half the couple, but Jared wasn't her partner. I didn't know who he was, since the back of his head faced me.

What was Amanda doing with him anyway? Wasn't it enough she had a new boyfriend? Did she really need to sneak behind his back with another guy? She made my stomach churn sometimes—partly because never in my reality would I have two guys at the same time.

I tiptoed toward the middle of the stage. A few steps from center, I let my shoes land hard against the wood floor, causing the sound to echo with authority. I planted my feet in a wide 'v,' folded my arms across my chest and glared into the pit.

"Hi, Amanda," I said.

"Brittany! You scared me."

"I've come to tell you I'm not going. Do you want me to tell Jared you're busy, or do you want to leave him hanging?"

Amanda and the guy squinted up at me. The light from my music stand lamp cast eerie shadows across their faces.

I turned on my heel. "I'll talk to you later."

"No, wait!" she said. "You have to come to Malley's. You have to."

"No, I don't," I said over my shoulder.

"But, look who I found. Kyle's coming with us. You have to come to even things out."

I turned in a slow half-circle to face them. Kyle gave me a sheepish grin before he ducked his head and ran his fingers back and forth on top of the pit barrier. I hoped he was feeling embarrassed over the fact that he and Amanda were going on a date at the same time she went with Jared. Did they want me to come and 'even things out' to keep Jared oblivious to the truth? I couldn't take any more of this.

"I'll see you tomorrow," I said.

"Brittany, get down here right now. You're coming with us to Malley's, and that's final." She turned to Kyle and said in a softer voice, "She has confidence issues. Tell her how much you want her to come."

"Amanda!" I threw her an icy glare.

Kyle's cheeks flushed. "I—um—I really would like you to come, Brittany."

"See?" said Amanda. "You can't refuse an invitation like that. You'll scar him for life. He'll never have the nerve to ask another girl out again. Do you really think you could live with yourself knowing Kyle will end up all alone in a cardboard box on the street somewhere?"

He raised his eyebrows and turned to her. "A cardboard box?"

"Just go with it," she said, nudging him with her elbow.

A few seconds later, after their snickers died down, she climbed the stairs to the stage and grabbed me by the arm. My resistance wasn't nearly as strong as it should have been. Someday I'd have to grow a backbone.

"We're all going together in Jared's car," Amanda said as she pulled me through the auditorium towards the exit door. "Don't forget to turn off that light, Kyle."

I ground my teeth together, steeling myself for an hour or two of pure torture.

We slurped down half our shakes while raising our voices over the clink of glasses and noisy chatter of the other diners. The four of us had reduced a huge plate of onion rings to almost nothing. One greasy ring lay among the crumbs, although the scent still floated in the air, mingling with the smells of fries and hamburgers from nearby tables.

Kyle reached for the last onion ring. Faster than an eighth note, I snatched it away. With a triumphant chuckle, I took a huge bite.

"Hey!" he protested.

"You snooze, you lose," I said with a laugh. I stopped chewing for a moment when I realized I was having a good time. Kyle didn't ogle Amanda, like every other boy in school. In fact, much to my surprise, I found his eyes resting on me way more than on her. When we sat down in the booth, he slid next to me without hesitation or a single wistful glance in Amanda's direction. Maybe she'd been right. Maybe he was interested in me.

I took a deep breath and back-pedaled a few feet. Kyle was an actor after all. He very well could be playing the role of the secret lover trying not to get caught by the jealous boyfriend.

Jared wasn't playing the part of the jealous boyfriend, though. He and Amanda sat close together on one side of the booth, but they didn't drop an invisible shield around themselves to keep everyone else out of their little romantic world. I'd been with Amanda plenty of times when that happened. From what I observed, most of Amanda's boyfriends guarded their time with her. Maybe they subconsciously knew their days were numbered.

Jared didn't seem to feel those insecurities. He treated me like a person instead of a threat. He and Kyle acted like best buddies instead of dueling rivals. They played off each other's humor, leaving Amanda and me so helpless with laughter we could barely sip our shakes.

Kyle grabbed the wrist of my hand that held the last half of the onion ring.

"That's my onion ring, and I'm taking it back," he said. He pulled my hand toward his mouth.

"No way." I protested as I fought a losing battle to regain control of my arm. "The onion ring is indisputably mine." I looked across the table, hoping to find support in the forms of Jared and Amanda. "You think it's mine, don't you?"

"I don't think it matters much what we think," said Amanda with a twitch of her eyebrows.

"No, no!" I laughed as my hand and the prized onion ring inched toward Kyle's open mouth. I pulled back on my arm as hard as I could. I was no match for his muscles. They seemed nice, but I didn't have time to admire them at the moment. I had an onion ring to win!

I couldn't let him beat me. As his teeth closed down on one end of the onion ring, I leaned forward and bit the other end.

What was I thinking? My impulsive move put my lips a fraction of an inch away from his. That's as close as two sets of lips can be without kissing.

My actions surprised Kyle as much as they did me. We both dropped our hands and pulled away. The bit of onion ring left out of our bites fell onto the red vinyl bench between us.

Amanda smiled sideways at Jared. "Too bad we're out of onion rings."

I couldn't look at anyone. I grabbed a napkin and became interested in wiping my hands. I'm sure my face blazed as red as ketchup. The next sentence out of Kyle's mouth was critical. He could either tease me mercilessly about trying to kiss him or pretend the whole thing never happened. Neither of those choices appealed to me.

"Okay, Brittany." My muscles tensed as he spoke. "The way I see it, you ate three-quarters of my onion ring. You owe me. Hand over your shake."

I laughed with relief and pushed the shake to him with the back of my hand. I wasn't about to fight for it the way I fought for the onion ring.

"All right," he said, twisting the cup in a careful inspection. "First we have to check for explosive devices. You can never trust an onion-ring-deprived girl to give up her shake without a weapon attached. Looks okay. You two didn't see her slip in any toxic substances, did you?"

Jared and Amanda shook their heads.

"Good. Now we have to get rid of the girl germs on the straw. Jared, do you have any disinfectant?"

"I never go on a date without it," said Jared. Amanda squealed and punched his arm.

"I guess I'll have to risk it," said Kyle. He took a sip and gagged.

I rolled my eyes. "Very funny."

"No, it's not the girl germs. What kind of shake is this?"

"Didn't you hear me order? Oh, yeah, you were filling the ketchup cups. It's bubble-gum-blueberry."

His head jerked back as his hands clutched his throat. "Are you out of your mind?"

"It's the kind I always get," I said, ducking my head.

"She got her first one when we were in second grade," said Amanda. I groaned as she geared up to reveal a silly tidbit from my childhood. One of the drawbacks of having a best-friend-for-life is she knows way too much about you. "We stood behind a guy who asked the workers to mix flavors for him. I think he wanted chocolate-marshmallow."

"It was chocolate-raspberry," I corrected.

"Whatever," said Amanda. "The point is, Brittany was fascinated by the idea of shakes with mixed flavors. And what two flavors do you think she chose?"

"Bubble-gum and blueberry," said Jared and Kyle in unison.

I buried my head in my folded arms on the table.

"Bubble-gum, for her favorite flavor and blueberry, for her favorite color. She's never ordered a normal shake since."

"It tastes good," I said without lifting my head.

"Right. You should see the looks she gets from the workers behind the counter. They always ask, 'Bubble-gum-blueberry? You sure?'"

"Not always." I raised my head. "Some of them are used to my order."

Amanda shook with laughter. "I'll never forget the time the girl behind the counter goes, 'You know, you can't return it if you don't like it.'"

"Well, I didn't want to return it. Here, Kyle, give it back if you don't like it." I grabbed my shake and spooned a big glob into my mouth. "Mmm-mmm."

"Disgusting," said Kyle. "Since I refuse to take that concoction as payment for my stolen onion ring, you'll have to pay me some other way."

"This is all I have left," I said as I held a dripping spoon out to him. He shielded his mouth with his hand.

"You can pay me back with a dance," he said.

"Fine. Catch me at the senior prom."

"I want to be paid now."

I choked on the spoonful of shake in my mouth. "Now?"

"Sure." Kyle scooted out of the booth.

"Here?" I asked.

"Why not?"

"Nobody dances here. There's no room. There's no music."

"There's music," said Amanda. "They play the radio over the speakers. If you listen, you can hear it."

I stuttered a few protests while Kyle pulled me to my feet.

"See, there's plenty of room." He swept one of my hands up in his and wrapped his other arm around my waist.

"What are you doing?" I asked.

"It's a slow song. Can't you hear it?"

I shook my head.

"Let me help." Kyle sang along in his fabulous voice. The song featured a female vocalist singing about the man she loved, but Kyle didn't seem to mind. He also didn't seem to mind that every set of eyes in Malley's zoomed in on us.

I couldn't stop laughing. I couldn't stop myself from trying to hide either. With the top of my forehead pressed against his shoulder, I used my free hand to veil the side of my face.

"You're spoiling the romance of the moment," he said in a scolding voice.

"Sorry. I didn't realize this was supposed to be romantic. If you'll let go of me, I'll ask the manager to dim the lights."

"That'd be great. Will you really?"

"Sure, but we'll have to wait 'til next time. The song's over."

"Is it?" He gazed up as if he could see the notes falling from the speakers overhead.

I slipped out of his arms and back into the booth, before he suggested we dance the next song. Rolling my eyes at Amanda and Jared, I said, "Drama people."

"Tell me about it," said Jared as he slung his arm around Amanda's shoulders.

Kyle slid back onto the bench next to me.

"I think my debt is paid," I said to him.

"All right. I'll let you off the hook, for now."

"Thank you very much," I said with a grin. My eyes locked with his for a few heart-stopping seconds.

"Brittany," Amanda said, breaking the spell. "Come with me."

"Where?"

She cleared her throat and lowered her voice a notch. "Ladies' room. Come on."

I smiled at Kyle. "Duty calls."

He stood up to let me out. "You girls never can go alone, can you?"

"You don't know what dangers lurk in the ladies' room. It takes at least two of us to fight off a glob of mascara in the sink or an empty perfume bottle on the floor."

"Sounds pretty treacherous."

I made a close pass by Kyle when I left the booth.

"Don't get lost," he said.

"Send a search party if we're not back in twenty minutes." I jogged around tables to catch up with Amanda, who stood at the restroom door. Once inside, she pulled a bulging makeup case out of her purse. She rifled through it while I finger combed my hair.

"You want to borrow my fuchsia lipstick?" she asked.

I crinkled my nose. "Huh?"

"Kyle looks good in it too."

"What are you talking about?" I asked, with one hand on my hip.

"When we go back out there, plant one right on his mouth."

"Yeah, right."

"I'm serious. Everyone in Malley's can see the two of you are dying to kiss each other."

I turned back to the mirror. "Don't let your imagination go crazy. Kyle's a nice guy. He's just being nice."

Amanda snorted out a breath of air. "He's totally got the hots for you! I told you last week, didn't I?"

"That doesn't make it true." I leaned close to the mirror and checked my teeth for stray crumbs.

"Okay, how about the facts, then? I've got proof he's in love with you."

"Really," I said with more than a hint of sarcasm.

"Yes, really." She tossed her eye liner into the makeup bag and zipped it shut. "Do you know what he was doing when I found him in the auditorium?"

I shrugged.

"He was putting something under your chair." She paused for dramatic impact. "A love note."

My heart skipped a beat. A note! My mind zoomed off in a direction opposite to the one Amanda intended. I found a note near my chair an hour earlier. Was this a habit with Kyle? I wouldn't have guessed a guy wrote the first note, but who knew? I suppose a fellow actor could become jealous of Amanda as easily as a girl watching her go through boyfriends. I wondered if the note Amanda received sounded like a guy wrote it. Maybe that's why she'd been leery of Jared.

"Listen, Amanda, you know that note..."

"Actually, it was more than a note. It was a small box, too. He hid it in his backpack, and denied having it when I caught him. I just know he was trying to give you a gift."

"Why would he do that?"

"Duh!" Amanda said, bulging out her eyes. "He's in love with you."

I pursed my lips. "He wouldn't let you see the box?"

"Nope."

"Did you try to look at it?"

"Yup. He threw it in his backpack and pretended not to know what I was talking about. Ah, the games we play for love." She fluffed her hair. "I'm going to go play some right now."

"Wait, Amanda, I want to see..."

She talked over my words as she headed out the door. "Remember, right on the mouth." She made a kissing sound as she left.

"Amanda!"

The door swung closed. I leaned on the sink and stared at my reflection. I wanted to like Kyle. He was nice and cute and fun. He seemed to have a spark of interest in me, too. But, was it all an act? Was it part of some diabolical plot? I shook my head. I'd been watching the play too much.

Something was not quite right where he and the notes were concerned, though. And a box.

That was weird. What was in it he didn't want Amanda to see? Did it contain something gross, like worms or a dead mouse? I'd have to put my heart on hold for a while until I figured it out.

I sighed. It figured. The one time I found a nice guy who seemed to like me, he turned out to be a psycho note writer. I had him for about an hour. That must have been some kind of record for me. Oh, well—easy come, easy go. Except it wasn't easy. A lump stuck in my throat as I walked out of the restroom.

Five

When I pushed through the restroom door, I saw Amanda pull Jared toward the exit.

"Get moving, Brittany, or you're going to get left behind," she said. I trotted over to the rest of the group.

"This was fun," Kyle said, looking at me. "We'll have to do it again sometime."

"Mmmm," I said, being as non-committal as possible.

"I can't believe it's this late," Amanda said as she herded us out the door. "I promised my mom I'd defrost the chicken for dinner. My dad's going to freak if we have macaroni and cheese again."

"Time flies," said Kyle.

We piled into Jared's car. Amanda tried to be sly, but I saw right through her. Every time she turned to talk to Jared, she sneaked a peek at me and Kyle in the back seat. What did she expect to catch us doing? We didn't provide her the slightest bit of entertainment. Kyle sat on his side of the car, as rigid as if he had a flagpole stuck to his back. I hugged the door on my side like a long lost friend.

Part of me wanted to be warmer to Kyle. Okay, a big part of me wanted to be warmer to Kyle, but I couldn't get the notes out of my head. Kyle wasn't the person he pretended to be at Malley's. He possessed another side he only allowed to come forth in dark auditoriums, near orchestra pits.

Amanda pulled the plug on her happy chatter. She rested her head against the car window, and her replies to Jared's comments became curt and guarded. She must have remembered the note Kyle slipped her. Of course, she didn't know Kyle wrote it, so she suspected everyone. I'd relieve her mind soon enough and let her go back to being at ease with her boyfriend.

But, how would she feel around Kyle? Angry? Afraid? Uncomfortable at the least. Her feelings would surely show through in her performance. Amanda was a great actress, but she wasn't that good.

I rubbed my eyelids. What should I do? Tell Amanda or not? Telling her would affect how well she acted, and she hated to perform at anything less than her best. If I didn't tell her, Kyle might continue to do whatever it was he planned to do. Why was he doing it anyway? I glared at him sideways through narrowed eyes. Did he want the play to be a flop? Or, did he want Amanda to be a flop? Was he worried she'd upstage him? He shouldn't have been. He was a great actor himself. When he sang with that caramely voice of his, every female in the audience would swoon.

Wait! Stop! I chided myself as a swoon of my own sneaked up on me. I massaged my eyes again. What was happening? How could I distrust this guy one minute and desire him the next?

Kyle's fingertips touched my cheek, making me jump. He rubbed softly for a few seconds.

"Your mascara smeared a little," he said with a smile as he dropped his hand.

My fingers rose to the spot where he touched me.

"Don't worry. I got it," he said.

I almost thanked him before I remembered what kind of a person he was. "I like to take care of my own face," I said.

His head snapped back an inch. He tried to smile, but he wasn't able to pull off his usual award-winning performance. "My compliments on a job well done."

I turned to the window as Jared pulled into the nearly empty school parking lot and rolled to a stop next to my lonely car.

"Thanks, Jared," I said as I opened the door.

"Yeah, thanks," said Amanda.

Jared put a hand on her arm. "Where are you going? I'm driving you home." His eyes shifted to Kyle and me before they rested back on her. "I thought Brittany could drop off Kyle..."

"It'll be easier if you take Kyle and I go with Brittany. She's coming to my house anyway."

"I am?"

"Remember?" she asked, nodding her head

and opening her eyes wide with encouragement. "You're going to eat dinner and study with me tonight."

My eyebrows scrunched together. "I don't remember—"

"We talked about this earlier. We're having your favorite, min-NOTE rice."

"Minute Rice? Oh, Minute Rice. Sure, I remember." Okay, call me stupid. Amanda wanted a chance to talk to me alone about the notes. She didn't trust anyone yet, including Jared, and needed an excuse to keep from being alone with him. It takes me a while, but eventually I catch on.

Had Kyle caught on to the min-NOTE rice hint? I glanced at him. He sat stone still, staring at the back of Amanda's head. That told me nothing, except maybe he liked Amanda's hair. Maybe he liked more than Amanda's hair. Maybe he liked Amanda. Well, of course he liked Amanda. He was a breathing, teen-aged male, wasn't he? Maybe he wrote the notes as a sick unrequited-love-revenge sort of thing. This guy was more messed up than I thought.

"See you tomorrow," Amanda said as she scrambled out of Jared's car. "Come on, Brittany."

"Coming!" I said as I grabbed my backpack. "Thanks for the ride, Jared."

"No problem."

Kyle leaned toward me as I climbed out. "Bye, Brittany."

I slammed the door on his words before I ran to unlock my car. When I looked up from the keyhole, I caught a glimpse of him through the back window of Jared's car as it pulled away. Kyle's whole face sagged. I knew he picked up on the arctic winds I sent his way—could he be moping because of me? A wave of doubt poured over me like a cloudburst. He seemed like such a decent guy. Maybe I judged him too fast. Could he have been doing something other than playing a cruel trick? I wished it were true with all my heart, even though my brain told me it was impossible.

My fist tapped against the top of my car as I

watched the red glow of Jared's taillights disappear. Why did you have to make me like you so much, Kyle?

"Let's go, Brittany. I'm freezing."

I gave my head a shake and climbed inside the car.

As soon as we arrived at Amanda's house, she sprinted for the kitchen to defrost some hamburger in the microwave. I guess she figured her dad would freak less over Hamburger Helper than macaroni and cheese. While she worked, I called my mom to ask if I could eat dinner with the Parkers. As Amanda dumped the thawed meat into a skillet, her mother came home and agreed to take over the browning and simmering chores. Amanda and I grabbed our backpacks and raced up the stairs to her room and some privacy. She slammed the door shut behind us and held out her hand.

"Let me see it," she said.

"The note?" My mind went blank. What did I do with it? I hadn't been too worried when I found it in the pit. I planned to throw it away. For the moment, I—

"Oh! Here it is." I dug the note from my pocket, and tried to flatten out the wrinkles on the one spot of Amanda's dresser that wasn't covered with cologne bottles or cans of hair spray. She snatched the note before I finished. Her eyes fidgeted over the words for a minute before she lowered the paper. Her whole body went limp.

"Why are you?" she asked.

"What?"

"Why are you friends with me? Everyone else hates me. Why don't you? Or do you?"

"Of course I don't hate you. You're my best friend. We've been friends forever."

"That's no reason to keep being friends. People change over time."

"We haven't changed that much," I said. I sat down on Amanda's bed, shoving aside the pile of throw pillows that covered half of it, and pulled her to sit next to me. "Who talked me into running away from home when I was nine, and my mom made me practice piano every day after school before playing Barbies?"

"Me," Amanda mumbled.

"Who tries to talk me into running away from reality by presenting me an endless list of boys she says are in love with me?"

"Hey..."

"You. See. Nothing's changed."

She twisted her lips, fighting down a smile.

"When we were in the fifth grade, who deemed herself my fashion advisor by telling me my pink flowered shirt didn't go with my green flowered skirt, even though they both had flowers?"

Amanda chuckled. "I remember that outfit. It hurt my eyes."

"And who, to this day, throws a stream of clothes over my dressing room door every time we go shopping?"

"I have a good eye for clothes."

"You do," I said. "You know how to look good. It's one of your many talents. That's your problem. You're good at too many things."

"Everyone's good at something. Why should I be picked on?" Her lips puckered in a pouty frown.

74

"Because you're good at highly visible things. You're good at looking gorgeous. You're good at flirting with guys. You're good at getting dates and boyfriends. That alone is enough to make us wallflowers mad with envy. Then you add your amazing voice and acting abilities—which we're forced to notice as you flaunt your goods across the stage during every school musical. It can be hard for some of us bland gals to take."

"Girls don't really feel that way about me, do they? It's silly."

"Never underestimate the teenage female's ability to covet."

"But...you. You don't feel like that."

I lowered my eyes. "Sometimes."

"Brittany!"

"I won't lie to you, Amanda. How can I not feel jealous?"

"Because you have so much more to offer than I do. You're good at tons of things I'm not. If you want to know the truth, there've been lots of times I've wished I were you."

"Not when you're in Jared's arms, I bet."

"Well..." She let her voice trail off before she giggled. "I do like the attention I get from guys."

"Jared wanted to give you a lot more attention than you let him this evening."

"I know. After I read that note, I couldn't trust anybody—except you."

"I think it's safe for you to trust Jared."

"Me too," said Amanda. She snatched her purse off the floor and rummaged through it until she found her note. "I think you're right about who sent these."

"You do?" I hadn't told her who I suspected. How did she figure out Kyle wrote the notes? "Yes. It has to be some girl who's jealous of me. Maybe someone who wanted the lead in the play and is mad because I got it. Or maybe it's someone who has a crush on Jared. Here, read the note I got. It makes sense."

I took the note from her with two fingers, as if it were covered with mold, and glanced at the words. Yep, same handwriting. I read it carefully.

You're perfect for this play.

Your acting is as big a joke as the script.

You sing worse than a donkey with a sore throat.

Kyle wishes you'd eat a breath mint before you kiss him.

Then, maybe he wouldn't puke after he does a scene with you.

Felicia won't survive the night. The pressure will crush her.

This was cruel. Whoever wrote this note had a warped brain. I mean, whose life was so meaningless they had to go around tormenting other people for kicks? I read the note again. And again. I smiled. I couldn't help it.

"What?" asked Amanda. "What's so funny?"

"Nothing," I said. I covered my mouth to hide my grin. The note writer talked about Kyle in the third person. He didn't write the notes! "Yes! Yes! Yes!" I fell backwards on the bed, bouncing with unquenchable glee.

"You seem pretty happy about this," Amanda said with a sneer.

"No, no," I said. I waved the note in the air. "This is awful. It's a terrible thing to do to you, and whoever did it is in serious need of counseling."

"You have a strange way of showing how upset you are."

"Look," I said. I sat up and pointed to Kyle's name in the note. "Kyle didn't write this."

"Of course he didn't. Why would he?"

"I found my note near my chair in the pit. When you told me you found him putting another note there, I just assumed..."

"But, it wasn't a note. It was a box with a note."

"I know. It doesn't matter anymore," I said with a shake of my head. I reached out and gave Amanda a hug. "He didn't do it. It wasn't him!"

"A-ha! I knew it. You tried to pretend you didn't like him, but I knew you did. He likes you too. It's so obvious. You two are the perfect couple."

"We're not a couple. But, I do like him." I bounced to my knees on the bed and grabbed

Amanda's hands. "Do you really think he might like me?"

"Absolutely."

"Don't say anything to him about me though, okay? Promise?"

"Who me?" she asked, batting her eyelashes in mock innocence.

"Please," I said. "I want to do this on my own. Do you understand?"

She stared at me for a moment before she said, "All right." She sparked back up a second later when she thought about her own boyfriend. "I'm glad I can relax around Jared again, now that we know the note writer is a girl with a grudge."

"Yeah," I said with a weak smile. A girl with a grudge. Was that something to relax about?

Six

Amanda crinkled her nose at the table covered with dirty dishes. "I guess we'd better get started."

She'd volunteered the two of us to clean up the kitchen after dinner. Her mom was beat from the tons of extra hours she'd spent working with the sewing committee lately, and she still had half-a-dozen chambermaid aprons to finish that night. Amanda's dad was in a grumpy mood at having to eat another pre-packaged meal. Her little brother and sister disappeared fast so they wouldn't have to help.

"It's not too bad," I said. "We'll be done in five minutes. Tops."

It took twelve and a half, but who was counting? What did we have to fill the rest of our evening with anyway? Sleep, homework, talking about boys…

The telephone rang.

"I'll get it!" Amanda said in her theater voice, which could startle a sleeping person on the last row of the auditorium.

"It's probably my mom telling me to come home," I said as I wiped the last spot off the countertop and threw the dishrag into the sink.

"Hello," Amanda said into the mouthpiece. "Hey! What's up?"

That didn't sound like her usual 'mom' greeting. I'd put my money on the returned-to-grace boyfriend.

"Is it Jared?" I asked in a whisper.

Amanda shook her head. Her eyes lit up, and she raised a finger in the air as if she had discovered the cure for pimples. With a jab, she turned on the speakerphone, sending Kyle's voice booming through the kitchen.

I covered my ears. "Turn it down."

Once she set the volume at a tolerable level, the reality of the phone call hit me. Kyle called Amanda. He wanted to talk to her. My instinct when I found them near the pit had been right.

He'd been interested in her the whole time and used me to get to her. The hamburger and noodles in my stomach turned to lead.

"I'm going home," I whispered to Amanda.

"Just a second." I heard her say into the phone. She covered the mouthpiece and whispered, "Wait. Listen to what he says."

Why should I? I was supposed to receive this phone call, not Amanda. I slumped down onto a bar stool at the counter and leaned my cheeks into my fists. Kyle's voice sounded as deep and rich over the phone as it did on stage. I listened with demented curiosity. I suppose I planned to replay the conversation in my head later, imagining I had been on the line instead of Amanda.

"Did she say anything to you?" Kyle asked her. "I swear, it was like someone flipped a switch and turned on a freezer."

"You must be imagining things," Amanda said with a wink in my direction. "Remember Malley's—the onion ring, the dance..."

My head snapped up. Were they talking about me? Had Kyle called to talk to Amanda about me?

"I don't know," he said. "I can't figure her out. I can't figure anything out."

"That's just love, dah-ling," she said. My heart stopped beating. How could she say that?

"I don't know about love." Kyle chuckled, sending my heart to my toes. "I don't know what I'm feeling, besides confused. Well, I'd better let you go. We both need our rest before the big opening tomorrow. Are you nervous?"

"But of course, my dear Edmond. Without fear of the unknown, life would be as simple and drab as a stroll through a park of grass and nothing but grass."

"Ooouuu," moaned Kyle. "I don't sound that bad when I say that line, do I?"

"It's not you. It's the line," said Amanda. "I hope the audience buys this play. If they start to boo, I'm hiding behind my big, strong leading man."

Careful, Amanda, you sound too flirty.

Kyle laughed. "No, we'll both jump into the orchestra pit."

"Yeah! They'll never find us there."

83

Right. Once you step into the pit you cease to exist.

"You're going to be great, Kyle. We both are. We'll be so good, we'll have every heart racing until the murderer is announced."

"I hope," he said. "You've made me feel a lot better. I'll have to call you more often."

"Anytime, big guy."

Big guy? Give me a break.

"Hey, well, I should go. Let's knock 'em dead tomorrow."

"You bet."

"Before I hang up, Amanda, will you promise me something?"

I leaned toward the speakerphone. Could this promise have something to do with me? Guys often ask a girl's best friend to put in a good word for them. Believe me, I know.

"What is it?" Amanda asked.

"Will you promise to leave the pink lipstick at home?"

"Awww." She faked a whine. "That scene won't be the same without it."

"I know. That's the idea. It will be much better if I'm not afraid to touch your lips with mine."

No, we can't have Kyle afraid to kiss Amanda. He has to make that kiss as long and passionate as possible. My teeth ground together.

"Okay, I promise," she said.

"See you tomorrow."

"Bye." She nestled the phone on its base and punched off the speakerphone with a beep. She turned to me, as pleased with herself as the star who squished the understudy back down to her place.

"I'm leaving," I said as I slid off the stool.

"You can't. That phone call is worth at least an hour's worth of re-hashing."

I let my head fall back and my shoulders slouch. "There's nothing to talk about, Amanda, and I don't feel like being here anymore."

"Kyle's right. You're on some sort of emotional rollercoaster. Do you think you might be manic?" She chuckled. "I think we should seek professional help."

I studied her face. She smiled, oblivious of

the pain she caused me.

"You know, I think you're right," I said, trying to sound calm despite the fact that my blood boiled so hot my skin should have blistered. "I do need to see a therapist. I must be crazy to believe a guy would choose me over you. You'd better order up a straight jacket. I'm definitely out of my mind. I am Amanda Parker's best friend. What sane person would put herself through such torture? Sometimes I come to my senses enough to ask—like the person who wrote the note—why am I your friend? You know I like Kyle. You encouraged me to like him. Yet, at the first opportunity, you throw yourself at him with everything you've got."

She looked like I'd thrown a rotten tomato at her.

"Well excuse me for trying to help," she said, lifting her chin an inch. "This is the thanks I get? I'm in the middle of the most stressful time of my life, and you're going to turn on me too? Tomorrow I open one of the trickiest plays I've ever done, and some maniac is trying to make sure I choke. I could've used some support from the only person I trust, but no. You decide it's time to perform the I'm-ugly-nobody-likes-me routine. I'm sick of the pity parties you love to throw for yourself, Brittany. Don't bother to invite me to the next one."

Steam shot out my ears and nostrils. "You are totally changing the subject. We're talking about your phone conversation with Kyle and how you flirted your head off the way you always do when there's a guy within fifty feet."

Amanda rolled her eyes. "P-lease."

"Isn't it enough you have a boyfriend? That you can get any guy you want with a twitch of your eyebrow? Do you have to throw yourself at the one guy I show some interest in, and who seems to have a teeny bit of interest in me? What are you trying to prove? Does it make you feel bigger to see me dateless on Saturday night when you're on your fifteenth boyfriend of the week?"

"You do need a straight jacket," Amanda said, her eyes narrowing. "Or maybe glasses. They might help you see the truth."

"I should've worn those glasses today at Malley's. Maybe they would have helped me see that Kyle is like every other guy. Brittany disappears as soon as Amanda's in sight." I dropped down onto a chair and buried my head in my arms on the table. "It's hard, Amanda. It's just so hard."

I heard the scratch of chair legs against the floor and felt the warmth of her hand on my back.

"You are an idiot," she said without the anger that laced her voice a moment earlier. "I know I've told you a thousand times, but you never listen. So, I'll tell you again. You're beautiful. You're attractive to guys. But, until you believe it, they won't either. Once you start to believe it, guys will run to your doorstep so fast, I'll be left standing on the street corner holding a sign that says 'Will work for dates.'"

I couldn't help snorting out a crying sort of chuckle. I raised my head, wiping tears away with the back of my hand. "It's a great picture, Amanda, but it's pure fantasy. How can I believe my life will change? Every conversation I have with a guy winds around to, 'You're friends with Amanda Parker, aren't you? Do you think you could introduce me?' I can't imagine anything else happening. I wouldn't know what to do if it did. And, when I'm stupid enough to believe a guy might actually be interested in me, I get plopped back into reality like a ripe peach onto concrete."

"You're right about one thing," she said. "You don't know what to do when something different happens. You're so set on being poor, lonely Brittany, you can't admit it's happening right now. Did you listen to one word Kyle said to me on the phone?"

"I heard him say he couldn't wait to kiss you in the play tomorrow and how he's going to start calling you all the time."

"Hell-o-o." She rapped her fist lightly against my head. "Is there a working brain in there? You don't need a straight jacket or glasses—you need a hearing aid."

"My hearing's fine, Amanda."

"Then the words got lost somewhere between

89

your ear and your brain. Since you missed the whole point of the phone call, I'll explain it to you very slowly. Kyle called me because he's crazy about you."

"Sure. That makes a lot of sense. Guys always call their girlfriend's best friend."

"You're such a hypocrite, Brittany! You just spent ten minutes whining about guys talking to you about me. Now you say it's impossible for it to happen the other way around? Come on, you're smarter than that."

I pressed my lips together as I mulled it over. "Maybe," I said, glancing sideways at her. "What did he say?"

She grabbed my hands as she scooted closer. "Okay. He's confused. He says you acted like you liked him one minute and couldn't stand him the next. I told him it was his imagination."

"It wasn't," I said. "And I wasn't acting. That's how I felt."

"Why?"

"Remember? I told you I thought Kyle wrote the notes."

"Oh, yeah. But, we know he didn't, so you're free to be yourself around him—like you were at Malley's with the onion ring."

"That was definitely not me," I said as I covered my face with my hands. I peeked at Amanda. "You think I have a chance with him?"

"I think you have more than a chance. I think you have him hooked. All you have to do is reel him in."

The telephone rang. I glanced at my watch. "Whoa, it's late. I'm sure that's my mom this time. Tell her I'm on my way home."

"Okay," said Amanda. She stood and lifted one hand towards the phone. "Good luck tomorrow."

"You too. I'm sure the play will be great."

"I'm not talking about the play."

I smiled and pointed at the phone. "You better get that."

Leaving her to make excuses to my mom, I darted out of the kitchen and through the foyer. As I yanked open the front door, I remembered my backpack. I jogged back a few steps and snatched it from the floor by the coat closet, where I set it before dinner. Before I stood up straight, the wind sucked the door shut with a bang.

"Hello." Amanda's telephone voice, or was it her theater voice, carried loud and clear to my ears from the kitchen. "Hey, Kyle, why are you calling me again so soon?"

I froze, my hand stuck to the doorknob as firmly as if it were coated with super glue.

"Guess what? She just left here—No. I know. Anyway, we're safe to talk freely now."

I didn't need to hear any more. I turned the knob and inched the door open enough to slip through. As I shuffled toward my car, a blast of cold wind nipped at my skin like a thousand tiny teeth, and whipped my hair like a dozen flailing arms. It felt good compared to the pain inside.

Seven

I twisted the dial on my locker to the correct numbers and pulled on the handle. No luck. I slammed my fist against the steel door. Wouldn't anything work for me ever again?

I turned the dial once more, holding my breath while I lifted the handle, as if my future happiness depended on my locker opening. Success! I reached for the plastic grocery bag that held my black clothes. I hadn't left my English class as early as I could have because Mrs. Morris was in the middle of a lecture on interpreting poetry that was important for an upcoming test. I wore black denims. All I needed to do was change into my black t-shirt, shoes and socks. I also needed to tune my cello. I had to hurry, or I'd miss the overture.

I tried to close my locker while shoving my

books onto the shelf and pulling out the bag. I ended up dropping my notebook and slamming the locker door on the bag. I tugged at the plastic handle in my fingers, as if I could pull my clothes through the crack. A groan slipped through my lips as I rested my head against the locker door. I might as well check out of school and go back to bed until spring. At least no one saw me humiliate myself.

"Hey, Brittany!"

I looked up and grabbed my locker handle to steady myself. Kyle waved and headed straight for me. An encounter with him was the last thing I needed. I turned to my locker and twisted the dial with shaky fingers.

"Having some trouble?" he asked.

"Nope," I replied as I focused on my locker. "And the name's Whitney."

He gave an uncertain chuckle. "No it's not, Brittany. Are you okay? Here, let me help."

Before I protested, he picked up my notebook. I reopened my locker and slipped out the plastic shopping bag without a word. He placed my notebook on top of my wobbly stack of books. I guess I shouldn't have put the smaller ones on the bottom.

"Whoa. Whoa!" he yelled as he tried to catch some of the half-dozen books that tumbled to the floor. I slammed the locker door in an attempt to halt the flow of books and papers, but it hit a book and bounced open. The contents of my locker covered the floor at our feet. We dropped to our knees to clean up the mess.

"I'm sorry. I'm such a klutz," he said while stacking the books in a sturdy pile. He placed them in my locker. "There you go, good as new," he said to my back. I decided not to move from my crouched position until he left. The muscles in my legs cramped. Why didn't he hurry and go? Instead, he picked up some papers.

"I can do it," I said. "You'd better go, or you'll be late for the play."

"I have plenty of time. I don't make an entrance until Scene Three, remember? I don't even get my turn in make-up until after the show starts. You, on the other hand, need to be performing five minutes before the curtain rises. Here." We both rose to our feet as he handed me my notebook with a trembling hand. What did he have to be nervous about? "Do you want this with your schoolwork?"

My eyes stared at the envelope he held. "Where did you get that?"

"On the floor with your other papers."

I snatched the note from his fingers and glanced at my name, printed in big black letters across the front of the plain white envelope. Not wanting to deal with it, I shoved it inside my notebook.

"We better head for the auditorium," he said. He grabbed my arm and pulled me down the hall. "The play starts in ten minutes."

"What?" The hall clock confirmed his statement and sent me into panic mode. "Wait!" I still held my notebook. I backed up a few steps, threw it in my locker and slammed the door shut before my books fell again.

"Let's go," said Kyle. He took hold of my hand and sprinted down the hall.

"Not so fast." My plastic bag bounced around my arm as I tried to keep up. We came to a corner, but did Kyle slow down like any sane person? Of course not. If anything, he increased his speed, running as if he were in contention for an Olympic medal. He took the turn on the inside, swinging me on his outstretched arm like the hammer in the track and field event. Momentum and gravity took over. Knowing my circular projection would end with a face-first crash into the wall, I squeezed my eyes shut.

Kyle caught me up in his arms as he continued the spin. I couldn't keep from squealing like a little girl swung in the air by her favorite grandpa.

"Kyle," I said through my gasps. "We're going to be late."

"They'll hold the show for us. They wouldn't dare start without the leading man and the leading cellist." He took my hand to begin our sprint again. I pulled back.

"I have to change," I said, pointing to the girls' restroom. I expected him to release my hand when I moved toward the door. He didn't.

"Guess I'll see you later," he said.

"I'll be in the pit, as usual. Break a leg."

"You too." As he dropped my hand, he leaned forward and kissed me on the cheek. Before I realized what happened, he turned and darted down the hall. My fingers rose to my face. He'd receive a gold medal if I were a judge.

Four and a half minutes later, I crossed the stage and climbed into the pit. The other members of the orchestra warmed up their instruments, but I barely heard them over the racket of the elementary students who filled the auditorium. The brass and string sections lifted my cello, passing it over their heads, to get it to my spot. I stumbled through music stands and over knees until I plopped into my chair.

Mrs. Fleming glared at me out of the sides of her eyes. I apologized with a nod of my head before I got busy tuning my cello. Everyone else was ready to begin. Mrs. Fleming forgave me enough to signal the first chair violin to give me a tuning note, and a whole minute to finish the process, before she began the overture. At her signal, we dived into the music and kept it afloat until the curtain rose.

Performing in front of an audience, even though it was a young and restless audience, made a difference. We were into it. The actors became their characters. The stage crew shifted and arranged the sets with the invisibility of a magician. The pit orchestra manipulated the audiences' emotions without them being aware we existed. We were good. The play actually worked.

Several minutes into it, when I had my first rest, Marissa nudged me. She pointed down with her finger and mouthed the words, "Look under your chair."

"What?" I mouthed back. She smiled and nodded. Since I didn't have to play again for several minutes, I leaned sideways, keeping my eyes on Mrs. Fleming to make sure she didn't notice my unusual movements. It was so dark, I couldn't see a thing. I felt around with my hand until it bumped into something hard. It was a box. It was *the* box. I pulled it out. Kyle had sneaked back to put it under my chair sometime after Amanda caught him yesterday. A fog of confusion muddled my mind. We ruled Kyle out as the note writer, didn't we? He couldn't have stuck a stink bomb or a dozen spiders under my chair.

I gulped as I ripped the lid off the small, brown box, curiosity overpowering fear. The darkness of the pit prevented me from seeing what was inside, until I held it close to my music stand light. I'm sure my toothy grin glowed in the blackness around me. One piece of bubble-gum and a scratch-and-sniff sticker with a cartoon blueberry, complete with face, arms and legs, lay in the bottom of the box. A typewritten note rested underneath them. I squinted to make out the words.

> *Will you come with me to Malley's after school for the real thing?*
> *I'm hoping we can get in another dance.*

The note wasn't signed. It didn't need to be. I savored the words as Marissa nudged me with her elbow. Mrs. Fleming stood poised, baton high, ready to begin the next number. I set down the box and positioned my bow in time to catch the first note.

Two seconds into the piece, my heart beat as fast as the tempo Mrs. Fleming flicked out with her baton. This song marked Kyle's entrance. Felicia and her uncle welcomed their hordes of house guests with a spirited song and dance number that contained several humorous and clever moments. The final guest to arrive was none other than the dashing Edmond, who caught Felicia's eye the moment he walked in. He caught my eye too.

Any time Kyle graced the stage with his presence, my mind drifted from my music. Once I played a song in the wrong key. A scowl from Mrs. Fleming yanked my attention off the stage and back into the pit. I had a hard time keeping it there, though. Kyle looked extremely handsome. I couldn't imagine a more gallant hero, as he strutted around in his costume defending truth and justice and romancing Felicia. He was good. Too good.

When Edmond made Felicia swoon, I swooned as well—and not with adoration. Kyle's attentions towards Amanda were too believable. He couldn't act the way he did on stage unless he had some real feelings for her. When I was with him in the hallway, I forced the previous night's phone call out of my head. The truth of it blared back as loud as if I stood next to the trumpet players. What did I have? A silly sticker and a piece of gum. Big deal. Amanda stood in his arms at that very moment, and in approximately twenty-eight minutes, they'd be locked together in a passionate kiss.

Edmond exited, leaving Felicia alone to sing a dreamy song about love. I played along, though my mind had gone numb. At the end of the song, I stared at the notes on the pages in front of me without seeing them. Marissa drew a sharp breath. I followed her gaze to the stage.

Felicia spent a good portion of the song dancing with a jacket Edmond left behind. She ended the song by putting on the jacket and hugging her arms around herself. She was supposed to discover a diamond necklace the murderer stole from her uncle in one of the jacket pockets. A trace of panic flashed in Amanda's eyes. The necklace wasn't there. DeDe waved wildly off stage, holding the necklace in her hand. But, Amanda couldn't walk over to get it without breaking character.

Without thinking, I started playing the last chorus of Felicia's song. Mrs. Fleming and the others picked it up a few measures later. Amanda repeated the chorus, modifying the dance steps to take her near the curtains at the side of the stage, where DeDe slipped the necklace to her. It was awkward, but not enough for the elementary kids to realize something had gone wrong.

Felicia found the necklace and the scene continued. Heartbroken to discover the man she had fallen in love with killed her uncle, Felicia threw an emotional fit. She picked up a pillow from the couch to throw across the room, but as soon as Amanda lifted the pillow, a stream of feathers floated from a large gash in the back. Amanda made the most of it. Hundreds of feathers swirled everywhere. Some floated into the pit. The stage crew would have an awful time cleaning them up in the thirty-four second blackout between scenes.

After she emptied the pillow and tossed aside the limp cover, Amanda reached for the cigar box she was supposed to throw to the ground. The box wouldn't move. Her eyes darted to the side as she tried to lift the box again. No luck. It had been fastened to the table. Without skipping a beat, she moved to the end table piled with a stack of books. Felicia was supposed to knock them to the ground with a wild sweep of her hands. Amanda swept and knocked, but, instead of pages flying, the entire table, with the books securely stuck together on top, bounced on the floor.

My eyes narrowed. Who did this? Of course I knew who, but I didn't know *who*. Felicia was supposed to rant some more before the scene ended, but when Amanda saw the table clunk to the floor with the books attached, she dropped to her knees to block it from the audience's view. She finished her tantrum with a fit of sobs on the floor before the curtain closed. I hoped Felicia was the one having the emotional fit and not Amanda.

When the curtains rose for the next scene, I saw Amanda offstage, waiting for her entrance. DeDe rubbed her shoulders and whispered encouragement. Amanda nodded as her eyes glazed over. Was she too rattled to pull this off? If her performance slacked, the whole play would fall apart. Elementary kids could be ruthless. If they lost interest in the play, we'd know it.

The next glitch happened a few minutes later. Felicia heard suspicious noises and went to explore a dark hall. She bumped into Edmond. Amanda reached for the sword she was supposed to pull from the display on the wall, to ward him off, but, big surprise, it wasn't there. Hmmmm. The props were being sabotaged. Maybe our note writer was part of the stage crew—a girl who had become attracted to Jared after working long hours with him.

Amanda improvised the rest of the scene without the sword. She pulled it off with seeming ease, but, after she exited, she collapsed into DeDe's arms. Amanda, limp as last week's flower arrangement, shook her head as DeDe gave her a pep talk. DeDe shook her a little as she held her by the arms.

Amanda straightened as Edmond made his exit. He didn't leave the stage at the scripted place. He exited at the spot where she stood and took her in his arms, talking to her all the while. She nodded and leaned her head against his chest.

They didn't notice, but DeDe gave them the dirtiest look I'd ever seen. What was her problem? It wasn't like the mess-ups were their fault. DeDe the Demented Director of Doom. She took her job as student director too seriously.

Kyle pushed Amanda away and held her at arms' length while he spoke soothing words. She finger combed her hair as she smiled up at him. The dashing hero jumps in to save the wilting heroine again. The show would go on. But, was my love life over before it began?

Eight

No other prop disasters occurred during the performance. When Amanda and Kyle took their final bows before the applauding audience, they beamed brighter than the stage lights. I couldn't tell if their grins were for the audience or for each other. I know they held hands on stage a lot longer than necessary.

I walked through the rest of the day in a daze. I caught the last half of lunch and pulled my brain together enough to stumble through my afternoon classes. As I gathered my books and stood to leave my last class, Ray, the guy who sat behind me, asked who died.

"Huh?" I asked, thinking I must look as sad as I felt.

"You're dressed like you're in mourning." With his pencil, Ray drew a line in the air from my shoulder to my toes. I glanced down. My mind was so numb I forgot to change out of my pit orchestra outfit. Oh well. The black clothes fit my mood.

Heading to the parking lot right after school seemed strange. I'd stayed late to rehearse for so long, I forgot about the traffic jam that happened there every day when the entire high school population tried to drive away at the same time. I couldn't even find my car for a while. When I did, and saw Kyle leaning against the hood, I wanted to bolt back inside the school.

A horn honked, forcing me to move forward. Was Kyle going to act like everything was great between us? I knew how I'd respond. I'd pretend I didn't see him. He'd get the message and back away as soon as my car moved.

He grinned as I approached. "Are you hungry?" he asked. He didn't think I was still going out with him, did he? I dropped my head and concentrated on unlocking my car door.

"Didn't you get my box? Hey, Brittany, are you okay?"

My hands shook so much I couldn't stick the key in the hole. Kyle nudged his way between me and my car.

"Are you mad at me again?" he asked.

I couldn't look at him.

"Will you at least tell me what I keep doing wrong?"

I pushed around him and fumbled with my keys. "Please don't play dumb with me."

"I'm not playing!"

"I don't want to talk about it."

Before I knew what was happening, he grabbed the keys, stuck the correct one into the hole and clicked open the door. Instead of dropping the keys into my outstretched hand, his fingers squeezed them more firmly in his own. He marched around the car, opened the passenger's door and slid inside.

"What are you..."

"I don't care if you don't want to talk. We need to. Get in."

I slumped into my seat and gripped the steering wheel with both hands.

"I'd appreciate it if you'd get out of my car," I said while staring out the front window.

"All right. But, I have your keys, so you won't get far."

I reached for the keys. He yanked them away and held them up high.

"I'm not in the mood to play games," I said.

"Good. Neither am I. I want you to tell me why you keep getting mad at me."

A gaggle of giggling girls passed my car. Their chatter slipped in and filled the empty space between Kyle and me. He leaned over to pull my door shut. The smell of his hair and the weight of his arm across my lap sent tingles down my spine.

No. No. No! I couldn't let my emotions take over. I needed rational thoughts now more than ever.

"We need to go someplace quiet. I'll give you your keys if you promise to go where I say."

I frowned and nodded. Kyle stuck the key in the ignition. Several minutes and many streets later, he instructed me to turn onto a long driveway. The lane wound through a tunnel of trees fat and full with the bright colors of fall.

He pointed to a parking spot at the edge of a large, empty lot. "Pull in here."

"What is this place?" I asked. I leaned over the steering wheel and peered out the window.

"It's a reception center. I came to my aunt's wedding reception here last spring." He hopped out of the car, jogged around to my side and opened the door.

I didn't budge. "I'm not going in there."

"We're not going in the building. I want to take you to a place on the grounds."

"What if someone sees us? We can't just wander around."

"Sure we can. Who's going to care? It's three o'clock on Wednesday afternoon. No one's having a reception. Come on."

He took my hand and pulled me out of the car. I accepted his help, but, when he shifted his fingers to get a better grip, I let my fingers slide out of his. My emotions with him had been up and down more times than a yo-yo doing the double gerbil. I couldn't stand the thought of one more downward spin. I decided not to let myself go up unless I was sure I'd get to stay there for a good, long time.

Kyle took my coolness in stride. We walked side by side, around the building, on a path through a clump of woods. When we broke through the trees, we stood on the edge of a wide lawn as lush and green as summertime. A pond with a small wooden building and waterwheel sat on one side. It was too perfect to have been there by coincidence. It had to be part of the landscaping for the reception center. I wondered how many hundreds of brides and grooms had posed beside it for a wedding portrait.

I didn't care if the slice of nature spread before me was man-made. It took my breath away. It was the perfect place to sit, relax—and share your innermost feelings? Is that what Kyle had in mind? Well, if that's what he wanted, that's what he'd get. I was ready to lay everything on the table and have a good, long look at it.

"A swan and her babies used to swim in this

pond," he said. "I suppose they've gone wherever swans go for the winter."

"Already? Too bad."

"I'll bring you back to see them next spring."

I glanced at him sideways. "Maybe."

We strolled near the edge of the pond until we arrived at a spot where large boulders lined the water—the perfect spot to sit and talk, or get a darling picture of the ring bearer and flower girl.

I climbed up on a rock, pulled my feet underneath me and hugged my knees to my chest. I gazed out over the pond, tilting my head at just the right angle to allow me to see Kyle out of the side of my eye. He kept shoving his hands in his pants pockets and pulling them out again.

"Is this quiet enough for you?" I asked without turning toward him.

He nodded and leaned sideways against the boulder. One hand stayed in his pocket, the other fiddled with loose bits of rock. "This is one of my favorite places. I've been back a lot since my aunt's reception. I've never wanted to show it to anyone else before."

"Why change now?" I asked.

"I've been thinking of bringing you here for the last couple of weeks, Brittany."

"Why?"

He let out a nervous huff of air. "Come on, you know."

"Spell it out for me."

"Okay. I l-i-k-e y-o-u."

"I bet you like a lot of people."

"Well, sure, but not..."

"Let's stop playing games, Kyle. I was at Amanda's house when you called last night."

He nodded. "She told me she turned the speakerphone on to let you hear."

"Not that phone call. Amanda thought I'd left when you called the second time. I heard what she said."

Kyle's lips twisted into a frown. "Then you know it was her idea."

"What!" Those were the last words I expected to hear. It was Amanda's idea? How could she do that to me?

He continued to talk, trying to explain himself while tripping over his tongue. "I'm not very good at coming up with creative ideas."

That's for sure. How much creativity did it take to fall in love with Amanda?

"The feelings behind it were mine though," he said. "And the idea of the box was mine to begin with."

My head jerked toward him. "What does this have to do with the box? Why did you give it to me anyway? As some sort of joke? I'll bet you and Amanda had a good laugh together backstage, thinking about my reaction when I opened it. Or were you too busy getting in some extra practice on your kissing scene? I thought Amanda was my friend, and I thought you—I thought you were..." I couldn't say another word. I lowered my head and buried my face in my arms and knees.

Several long minutes passed. Kyle stood so quiet, I wondered if he had sneaked away. I froze when I heard him climb onto the boulder. The warmth of his arm seeped into mine where they touched. He sat still for a long time, making me wish I could slide off the rock and disappear into the pond.

"I thought *I* was confused," he said. "Did you really hear my second phone call with Amanda?"

"I heard enough," I mumbled through my knees.

"Tell me exactly."

I turned my head, so I could see a slice of him, and sighed. "Amanda told you I was gone and you didn't have to pretend anymore."

"Pretend? Pretend what?"

"Pretend—you know—that you aren't together. As a couple."

His eyebrows scrunched together. "Are you sure she was talking to me?"

"Yes. Actually, I think what she said was, 'We're safe to talk freely.'"

"Oh." He nodded. "Did you hear anything else?"

"I didn't need to, so I left."

He let out a soft chuckle. Boy, this guy was sick if he looked to my shattered emotions as comic relief.

"You left before we got to the good part, Brittany. I know you know Amanda caught me trying to put a box under your chair in the pit yesterday. I pretended she was wrong because I was embarrassed. The box was a stupid way I thought up to tell you I wanted to get to know you."

I must have looked ridiculous with my mouth hanging open as wide as if I sat in a dentist's chair. He didn't seem to notice and kept explaining.

"Amanda rejected my original idea of leaving a note from a secret admirer and a bag of M&M's under your chair. She was right. The note would be silly now, since you'd know who sent it. She also told me you don't like M&M's. We shot ideas back and forth, trying to think of something meaningful I could leave you. I wanted to remind you of the fun we had on our first date, and Amanda came up with the gum and sticker idea."

"Is that really what happened?"

"Really."

"The way you and Amanda were talking, the

117

way you act around each other, the way you kiss on stage..."

"We're friends, Brittany. That's it. And what happens on stage is what's known as acting."

I studied his eyes while a cool breeze pushed his hair back and forth across his forehead.

"Can you honestly say you're not attracted to Amanda?" I asked. "Every other guy in school is. It's only natural. I mean, I wouldn't blame you. She's gorgeous."

"She's not the only one." He took my hand in his. His fingers shook as much as mine, but they all settled down after a few seconds. "I'll admit Amanda is nice looking and fun to work with in the play, but I've never had any romantic thoughts about her. Besides I never date anyone I'm working with in a play. A certain someone is still fuming about that, but it makes things too complicated and could spoil the show. It's a strict rule for me."

Rules! I sat back, snatching my hand away.

"I have rules too, and I think you break several of them."

"Like what?" he asked with a nervous half-smile.

"I can't date someone who's dated Amanda. I know you went out with her at least once after rehearsal."

He sucked in a deep, easy breath. "Those weren't real, planned-ahead, one-on-one dates. A whole group of us from the play went out together a couple of times. I don't think I even sat by Amanda. Anything else?"

"I can't kiss anyone who's kissed Amanda."

Kyle raised his right hand as if swearing an oath in court. "I have never kissed Amanda. Ever."

"I've seen you do it dozens of times."

"No, you've seen Edmond kiss Felicia. That's totally different."

I bit my lip while I mulled it over. I figured I could let the kisses slide, since they were stage kisses.

"I won't date anyone Amanda wants to set me up with. She's the one who first told me I should think seriously about you."

"That doesn't count," he said, waving his hands. "I became interested in you on my own. Amanda was just smart enough to pick up on it and spill it to you."

"Well, all right." I took a deep breath. "There's one more."

"Shoot."

"I need to know the truth on this one, even if you think it's going to hurt me."

"Okay," he said.

My words came out in a guarded whisper. "Are you using me to get to Amanda?"

"What?" He sat up straight.

"It's happened before. A lot."

"Why would I do that? If I've done anything, it's been the opposite. I've used Amanda's friendship to get to you."

"Promise?"

"Um-hm. Are we done with these silly rules now?"

"Yep." I smiled for the first time that afternoon.

"Are you done being mad at me?"

"For now," I said with a laugh.

"Good. Because whenever I think of bringing you here, there's something we always do."

He leaned close. My heart beat so fast I was sure he could hear it. I didn't breathe as his lips pressed against mine. When the kiss ended, and I was able to catch my breath, I found his arm around my shoulder. I leaned my head against him and sighed. I admit it. I was in paradise.

Nine

"I thought rehearsals were over," Brooke said as I entered the kitchen through the door from the garage.

"They are." I dropped my bulging backpack onto the counter and stuck my chin over her shoulder to peer into the frying pan on the stove. "What's this?"

"Dinner," she replied as she nudged me back.

"Smells good. What is it?"

"One of those frozen stir-fry things."

"Where's Mom?"

"Locked in her room with her laptop. She said she had to get her e-mail out before six-thirty. That's why I got stuck with kitchen duty." She gave me a skillet-hot glare. "You should be doing this instead of me, since you didn't have rehearsal. I've carried way too much of the load around here lately."

"I know. It's true." Not letting her cranky mood affect me, I wrapped my arms around her. "Thank you. You're wonderful. The play will be over soon, and I'll be able to do my share."

"Cut it out," Brooke yelled as she slapped my hands.

I hummed and turned in a circle, bringing her with me. "Come on, Brookie! It's a glorious day. Don't be a sour puss."

"What's with you?"

"Nothing. I'm wonderful. The world is wonderful."

Wrenching herself out of my arms, she turned to face me, spatula ready to defend herself. "What's going on? Why are you so late getting home from school if rehearsals are over? Where have you been?"

"Oh, nowhere," I sang.

"Is this about a boy? Did you get lip or something?"

I froze. "Did I what?"

Brooke inched forward and dropped her voice. "Did you get lip? You know, kissed?"

My head fell back while I laughed. "Interesting way of putting it." I grabbed her hands, including the spatula, and pulled her forward to confide my secret. "I did kiss someone today. Someone unbelievable." I threw our arms in the air, as I spun away on my toes like an overgrown ballerina. When I stopped, I found Brooke smiling.

"Can you believe this is happening to me, Brookie?"

Her eyes sparkled. "Is he cute? And nice?"

"He's gorgeous. And talk about nice. He surprised me with a present under my chair in the pit today. And we drove to the most romantic spot after school. It's too good to be true. I hope I'm not dreaming. I'm not dreaming, am I? Pinch me—no, don't pinch me. If I'm dreaming, I don't want to wake up."

"You're not dreaming," said Brooke. She sniffed the air for half a second before she whirled back to the stove and scraped at the food in the skillet. "You can smell dinner burning can't you? Food never burns in dreams."

"Augh!" I laughed as the high-pitched scream

of the smoke detector wailed in my ears.

"Turn it off!"

"Okay, okay." I pulled a stool underneath the smoke detector attached to the ceiling. The noise didn't stop until I pressed the button several times. "At least Mom won't ask you to cook again for a while."

"Whatever I have to do to get out of it."

"What's going on?" Brianna asked as she entered the room. "Where's the fire?"

"You heard the alarm," I said. "Why aren't you next door calling 9-1-1?"

"I figured it was a small stove top fire, since Brooke is cooking."

"Very funny," said Brooke. "Guess what, Bree. Brittany has a boyfriend."

"A real one?" Brianna asked.

I placed my hands on my hips. "What other kind is there?"

"Imaginary," said Brianna.

"Well, this one's real," said Brooke.

"Who is he?" asked Brianna. "What's his name?"

"His name is Kyle. And, if you come to the show, you'll see how fantastic he is. He plays the lead."

"I thought Amanda was the lead," said Brianna.

"She is," said Brooke. "She's the female lead. Every female lead has a male lead. Does your boyfriend like Amanda in the play?"

I nodded. "His character falls in love with her character. They even kiss."

Brianna's eyes bulged. "Your boyfriend kisses Amanda?"

"It's not a real kiss, Bree. Everything in a play is pretend."

"Still, doesn't it make you mad to watch him kiss her?"

"It used to, but I'm okay with it now." I paused and smiled to myself, realizing I *was* okay with it. The play would be over in three days. Kyle's lips would soon belong to me alone. When that time came, I wouldn't play nice and share them with anybody else.

A new hope danced in my sisters' eyes, as

they stared at me with faces almost mirror images of my own—not that we looked like triplets born at different times. We were more like variations on a theme. I attended a symphony concert once that included a rendition of "Twinkle, Twinkle, Little Star" played in many different styles. That's what my sisters and I were, each a different style of "Twinkle, Twinkle, Little Star." Brooke was definitely country—emotional and forlorn at times, and downright silly at others. Brianna was a version in the style of Irish dance music—pulsating with life and energy. I think I'd have to be the classical style, full of trills and runs, supported by chords with so many tones it's impossible to hear them all. I was only beginning to discover some of those tones myself.

"Which night is the family coming to the play?"

"I don't think we've decided yet," said Brooke.

"We'll definitely come see Kyle," said Brianna, bouncing on the balls of her feet. "Do you think he'll ever come over here?"

I couldn't help smiling. "I won't let him set one foot through the door. The second he sees you two, I'll lose him forever." I reached out and grabbed Brianna with one hand and tickled her with the other. She screeched in delight, more at my words than the tickling. I got in a few teasing pokes to Brooke's stomach while I was at it. She tried to act cool, but she couldn't hold down her smile.

Brooke cleared her throat and turned back to the stove. "Will you guys quit clowning around and set the table? This food is more than ready."

"You do the table, Bree. I have to take my stuff to my room. I'll unplug Mom while I'm up there and bring her down."

"Okay," Brianna agreed. My good mood must have infected everybody. Brianna didn't normally do a chore without at least ten minutes of whining first.

I gathered my backpack in a bear hug and trudged up the stairs. I had to designate the rest of the evening as serious homework time. The play had drained a large and constant flow of study hours from my schedule over the past few weeks. My GPA was caught in the downward spiral of a whirlpool and on the verge of drowning. If I scrambled, I could resuscitate it before the term ended and official report cards came out. I'd lock myself in my room with my books after dinner and not come up for air until bedtime—although I might be persuaded to take a break if I received a phone call from a certain actor friend of mine.

I rapped on Mom's bedroom door with the back of my knuckles as I passed.

"Dinner," I called through the wood. I heard the clicking of the keyboard.

"Five minutes," she called back.

"All right, but not a second more." I moved down the hall, kicked my bedroom door open and heaved my backpack onto the bed. I had five minutes. I decided to make the most of it by organizing the tidal wave of homework I had to swim through. I grabbed a pencil and flipped open my notebook.

An envelope fell onto the bed. I gulped. The excitement of the day made me forget I had received another note.

Pictures of Amanda struggling on stage, which I'd squeezed out of my memory while it was filling with Kyle, flicked back onto the screen of my mind in full color. I made a mental note to give her a supportive phone call later.

The performance had been rough, but Amanda had pulled through. Maybe her determination to stay calm would discourage the note writer from doing anything else. I hoped so.

We would perform the play for our school the next day, followed that night by our first performance in front of a real, grown-up audience. I'd love to figure out the identity of our friend with the poisoned pen and make sure she's far away from the stage long before the curtain rose at the matinee. I tore open the envelope, hoping beyond hope the writer revealed a clue about her identity.

> *What happens to Amanda today is nothing.*
> *Only her pride will get hurt.*

The real fun begins soon.

Abandon her or face the same fate...

The note revealed only one clue—the person who wrote it was crazy. I crumpled the paper between my fingers. A psycho was loose at our high school, and she was starting to scare me. I had to talk to someone immediately. My thoughts flew to the strongest, bravest hero I could ever want—Kyle. But, Amanda made me swear not to tell anybody. Okay, Miss Felicia, you'll have to hear my worries yourself.

I raced to the phone in the hall, grateful to see Mom's door open. That meant she'd finished her e-mail and had gone downstairs. She wouldn't overhear my conversation—which would throw her into a hissy fit that would result in my being forced to quit the play and call the police.

Ignoring Brooke's yells that dinner was getting cold, I punched in Amanda's number.

"Start without me," I shouted down the stairs. "I'll be there in a minute."

I worried over leaving Mom alone with Brooke and Brianna and the knowledge they possessed about Kyle, but it was a risk I had to take. I'd have gushed out every detail to Mom before dessert anyway.

"Hello, Parker residence."

"Hi, Mr. Parker. This is Brittany. Is Amanda there?"

"No. You know she won't be home for another half an hour. Why aren't you at rehearsals?"

"Excuse me?" I asked.

"They let the orchestra go early, eh?"

"Uh..." My mind whirled with the implications of Mr. Parker's words and the various reasons Amanda might have lied to him about rehearsals. I was torn between blurting out the whole situation to the wise, solid fatherly figure on the phone and talking things over with Amanda first to find out what was going on.

"She's expecting me to pick her up at the school in twenty minutes. I'll have her call you when she gets home."

"Hey, do you know what, Mr. Parker? I

planned to swing by the school to get a book I forgot. Do you want me to get Amanda while I'm there? It'd save you the trip."

"You're going there anyway?" he asked.

"Yeah." As of fifteen seconds ago.

"Well, sure. Be in front of the school by seven. You know, you're helping me save gas. We have to think of the environment, don't we?" He chuckled.

"That's right. I'll bring her straight home."

"Great. I appreciate it, Brittany. Good-bye."

"Bye."

I dropped the phone back in the cradle. *Amanda, what are you doing? If it's something flaky, I'm not going to cover for you.* I told myself Amanda was sneaking in an innocent date, but the words of my most recent note kept flashing through my mind. What if the note writer lured Amanda to the empty auditorium? What nasty surprise did she have waiting for her? *I'll be there soon, Amanda. Hang on.*

Ten

I took two minutes to eat dinner. It wasn't hard to skimp on the serving size of Brooke's overdone stir-fry, and no one blamed me for not eating much.

The gas pedal stayed close to the floor of the car all the way from my house to the school. I prayed I wouldn't be too late.

A slippery, cold hand tickled the inside of my stomach as I screeched to a stop in the principal's parking space, the closest one to the front door. I knew none of the faculty worked that late and no one would tow my car away for illegal parking, but leaving it in the forbidden spot made me feel like a thief sneaking away from the scene of a crime.

I ran up the walkway to the front entrance of the school. A blanket of blackness covered the grounds and building, except for the yellow circles of street lamp light and the inadequate safety lights illuminating the entryway and front halls of the school. The sound of my feet pounding against the cement echoed back to me.

I couldn't see anyone. Amanda told her dad to pick her up at seven. She wouldn't stand him up like she often did me, would she? I pictured Amanda batting her eyelashes at her father. He was a grade 'A' lobster: tough as nails on the outside and marshmallow cream on the inside. She could get away with anything.

I arrived a few minutes early. Amanda could still show up. The thought didn't calm me. The image of Amanda lying hurt somewhere inside the building wouldn't budge from my mind. I jumped up the small set of steps in one stride. Two more strides placed me at the glass front doors. I yanked at the closest one. It clattered but didn't open. None of the doors opened. My fists pounded against the glass while I yelled.

"Hello! Is anyone in there?" Not a single shadow twitched. I leaned my forehead against the glass. Why was I here? I needed to be home spending quality time with my schoolbooks instead of rushing to rescue my best friend, who was probably nestled in the arms of our stage crew director at that very moment.

"Brittany? Is that you?"

I squinted into the darkness. A form huddled against the wall next to the glass doors.

"Amanda! What happened?" I lunged forward, skidding to the ground next to her. "Are you okay? Did she hurt you?"

She raised her head, her tear stained cheeks visible in the dim, yellow light.

"It's all right. I'm here now." I patted her back. "Tell me what she did to you."

Her forehead crinkled. "She?"

"The note I got from her today totally freaked me out. I almost died when your dad told me you were at rehearsal. I rushed right over. How could you let her lure you here alone?"

"This has nothing to do with the notes," she said with a shake of her head. She blotted her eyes with the back of her sleeve and sniffed. "Jared and I wanted to go out. I'm so far behind in my homework, Dad never would've let me. So I lied to him. Jared wasn't worth it. He turned out to be a jerk like all the others." She covered her face with her hands.

"What happened?"

"It's like they don't even want to take the time to get to know me." She dropped her hands and let her head fall back against the brick wall. "They only care about one thing."

"Who?" I asked.

"All of them. All my boyfriends. That's why I dump them. It's just that I liked Jared so much!"

I sat back. "I don't get it. If you like him, why did you break up with him?"

"It's kind of like a rule for me."

"Don't tell me you have rules too," I said with a groan. "Forget them. They're probably as silly as mine. I let them slide for Kyle. Maybe you should let yours slide too."

"Brittany, I can't believe you'd say that."

"Why? What's the rule?"

"If they want too much too fast, they're

history. It shows they only care about the way I look."

"Is that really so bad?" I asked. "I wouldn't mind a guy being crazy about my looks."

"You would if that's *all* he cared about," she said, scowling. She closed her eyes. "What do I keep doing to make them think I'm so easy?"

"You're not doing anything." I made her look at me by giving her a playful shove. "Unless you want to grow your hair over your face and stop showering, you can't blame yourself for being irresistible."

"You'd think they'd show some self-control," she said as she rolled her eyes. "I mean, what makes them think I'd go that far on the first or second date?"

I lowered my voice a few notches. "How far?"

"A heavy-duty, groping make-out session is too far for me; I don't care how long I've been going with a guy. And they think I want it on the first date? Give me a break. For once I'd like a boyfriend who wants to spend our first date talking and maybe holding hands. I'd love it if he waited for the second date before he kissed me."

I did some quick calculating. Did the onion rings at Malley's count as a first date? Then the reception center was date number two. Good. We were right on track, except for the hand holding. We didn't hold hands on the first date, and only did a little on the second. Oh, well. We'd get more of that in later. What else would we get in later? I'd never been close enough to having a boyfriend to have to worry about what to do with him once I had him.

"So what do you do when a guy starts pushing too far?" I asked. "You don't dump him on the spot, do you?"

"He gets a warning. Sometimes two. But, I swear, it's like they start to think in opposites. 'Stop it' means 'come on.' 'That's enough' means 'give me more.' 'I'm leaving' means 'come and get me.'"

I shook my head in amazement. "This is why you break up with all your boyfriends?"

"It happens like clockwork."

"Why haven't I heard any of this before?" I

asked. "I thought we told each other everything."

"Don't get mad, but you do tend to freak out when it comes to me and boys."

I gave her a meek shrug. "I'll give you that."

"I'm not totally insensitive to your feelings. If you knew I dumped boys because they wanted too much, when you couldn't find one to give you anything—well you know what that would do to you. Since Kyle's panting at your doorstep now, I think you can handle it."

"Thanks," I said, giving her arm a squeeze. "It's probably a good idea to set limits. I'll have to talk to Kyle about that." I fiddled with the zipper on my jacket. "I'm sorry I misjudged you. I guess thinking you were flaky made it easier for me to watch you go from one boyfriend to the next."

"Sometimes I wish I were a flake instead of a prude," she said with a hint of a smile. "Hey! Did you say something about Kyle? Did you finally work things out with him?"

"Yes." I grinned. "Thank you for your role as romantic advisor. The box under my chair was a nice surprise."

140

"Does that mean the two of you are together?"

"Yes!" I said, unable to keep myself from adding a little-girl squeal. "We are together. Can you believe it?"

"Of course I can believe it." She snorted a small laugh. "How the tables have turned. Here you sit with the perfect boyfriend, while I'm lonely and single."

I leaned forward and gave her a hug. Maybe I shouldn't have, because she started to cry again.

After I climbed to my feet, I grabbed her arm and pulled her up. "Come on. Let's go home."

"Why did he have to do it?" she asked. "We always had so much fun. And we looked cute together. Don't you think we looked cute together?"

"You'll look cuter with the next guy. I promise."

Amanda shook her head. "I don't want a next guy. I'm sick of the whole business. I'm going to quit dating until I'm ready to get married. You have a boyfriend. I can live my social life vicariously through you."

"Yeah, sure. Come on."

She stopped walking halfway down the path

and tightened her hands into hard fists. "He was perfect!"

"Amanda." I grabbed her shoulders and turned her to face me. "If he's so great and you like him so much, why don't you give him another chance? Everyone makes mistakes."

"Nope. Can't. It's..."

"One of your rules," I finished for her.

"I wish I could. I need an ally backstage. You saw what happened to me today. I'm almost afraid to go on tomorrow. I found another note stuffed in my locker. It's vicious, Brittany."

"What did it say?" I asked.

"Read for yourself." She pulled the note from her back pocket and flung it at me. I held it sideways and tilted my head to see the words in the dim light. I should have left them in the dark shadows where they belonged.

Felicia, beware ...
Prop daggers cut.
Falling scenery crushes bones.
Cinched costumes cut off air.

Misplaced steps lead to PITfalls.
Stage kisses are full of venom.
A short in the mic is a hair-raising feeling.
Jealous cast members wait to pounce.
Will there be another corpse on stage?

"Wow," I said. "This is ugly."

"No kidding. What did your note say?"

Amanda couldn't handle the details at the moment. She didn't need to read the nasty threats written to her again either, so I shoved her note into the pocket of my black jeans.

"My note had basically the same message as yours," I said. "What should we do? I think we should tell someone."

"We have no clue who's doing this. All the principal or Mr. Elliot could do is postpone or cancel the play."

"Maybe shutting down the play is best," I said, willing to give up sitting in the pit while my boyfriend (MY BOYFRIEND! I couldn't believe I could say those words!) kissed Amanda onstage.

"No way. Too many people have put in too

143

many hours on this stupid play. We're bound and determined to prove good acting can save the corniest script. We can't let this psycho win, Brittany."

"But, she's serious. She already carried out some of her threats."

"I'll handle whatever she throws my way."

I sighed, knowing I was defeated. "I don't want to see you get hurt."

Amanda's eyes fixed in a steady and somber gaze. "After what Jared did to me today, I can't be hurt any worse. Believe me."

Eleven

I bowed out deep, rich notes, focusing on the music as I hadn't been able to for a while. I sat in the pit with the other orchestra members, rehearsing the music we—okay I—flubbed during the performance for the school.

When I climbed into the pit before the show, I checked my music folder and stand for messages. I don't know if I was relieved or disappointed not to find any. After I warmed up on my cello, I settled in for the performance. As the house lights dimmed, Marissa handed me an envelope.

"Who gave this to you?"

She shrugged. "No one. I saw it on the floor."

I couldn't wait the precious minutes until my first break to read the note. With my cello resting against my shoulder, I ripped open the envelope. Mrs. Fleming lifted her baton, ready to start the number at any moment, while I yanked out the note. It took two seconds to read. The only words written were, *tonight—tonight—tonight*. I glanced around and found a set of eyes staring straight at me. They belonged to L.J., the last person in the world I'd suspect. He didn't blink. He must have been gauging my reaction to the note. Wait. Were his eyes settled on me or—I glanced to my right—Marissa?

Mrs. Fleming's hand whipped through the air, starting the song. Fumbling with my bow, I jumped into the number. Needless to say, my entrance wasn't without a few splashes. Mrs. Fleming gave me a deep frown. I don't suppose I'll get invited to participate in a pit orchestra again.

When Amanda made her first appearance, Marissa let her bow go slack and leaned toward my ear.

"She is *so* gorgeous," she whispered. "I'm either going to have to kill her or kill myself."

"Very funny," I said, pretending to laugh. We went back to playing, but my eyes kept darting between the sheet music and Marissa's face. Had she been joking? She could have slipped me the notes in the pit easier than anyone. L.J. wouldn't have had a problem planting them either.

Amanda's confident voice belted out the words to her first solo. My heart raced. Her portable mic cut in and out all through the song. The note writer must have messed around with it.

Uncle Conrad came on to join her in the number. His mic didn't work at all at first. A moment later, when he spoke, he tried to talk extra loud. His mic started cutting in and out while he said, "This is my lovely niece, FELICIA. TAKE INSPECTOR TISDALE TO his BEDroom, Miss Kline." A wave of snickers flowed through the audience. The mics had problems like that all the time. I'd forgotten some stage disasters were a matter of course, and not a matter of psychopaths.

With all the thoughts running through my mind, I couldn't play my best. I did an adequate job until the kissing scene. I thought I'd be okay with it, but seeing Kyle's lips—the lips that touched mine less than twenty-four hours earlier—make contact with Amanda's lips made me want to jump on my chair and howl like a crazed werewolf. Don't try to tell me it was Edmond kissing Felicia. When I saw the two of them kiss, my brain refused to believe it was pretend. My mistakes weren't blatant, but they were enough to draw Mrs. Fleming's attention to me yet again.

After the last curtain call, Mrs. Fleming held the members of the pit orchestra in place with a flat palm hovering over us. Once the auditorium emptied, she announced an extra rehearsal, compliments of yours truly, to make sure we—okay, I—was prepared for the performance that night.

With my eyes and mind on the music, I allowed myself too be pulled into the harmony I provided. I played well, and the rehearsal didn't last long, just long enough for the crew to finish setting up the props and scenery for the next show. They left the stage dark and deserted.

As the other orchestra members climbed out of the pit, I ran over some tricky spots in the music one more time. I enjoyed playing in the pit orchestra. I loved how music added a deeper level to the action on stage. The musical in the spring would be my last chance to be in a high school pit orchestra, and I didn't want to miss out on it. As the last of my fellow musicians crossed the stage towards the hall to the orchestra room, I inched toward Mrs. Fleming to apologize.

"I lost my concentration today. I'm sorry. It won't happen again." I blinked my eyes with great seriousness.

"See that it doesn't," she said. "I need you in this orchestra. I'm not the only one who's noticed you're distracted. I don't know what I'd do if they removed you."

"Has Mr. Elliot said something about me?"

"No, it was that student director—what's her name?"

"DeDe," I said. The Demented Director of Doom.

"That's right," said Mrs. Fleming, snapping her fingers. "She's a bit intense, isn't she? Well, I wouldn't worry too much about her—if you pull yourself together." A small grin appeared on her face. "He *is* handsome."

"What?" I couldn't believe what I was hearing.

"The leading man, Edmond. Quite a ladykiller, wouldn't you say?" She leaned over her stand. "The young man who plays him is something to write home about as well."

"Mrs. Fleming, I don't know what you're—"

"I can see what's going on as well as the next person. Leaving gifts under your chair, stealing glances at you from the stage. I know when romance is blowing in the air."

I'm sure my cheeks looked as red as if they'd been painted for the play.

Mrs. Fleming pointed her baton at me. "He's a nice young man, Brittany, but, leave your feelings for him outside the pit. All right?"

I nodded. "I will. I promise."

"Good. I'll see you tonight." While Mrs. Fleming climbed the steep steps out of the pit, I went back to collect my cello, bow and music folder.

So much noise and commotion usually bounced around the auditorium, it sounded eerily quiet when I stood there alone. The lights still shone over the rows of seats, but the stage stood dark and silent. I snapped off my music stand light and wound my way through the chairs and up the stairs.

My steps turned into shuffles. I could see well enough while I crossed the stage, but, after I walked through the black curtains, the auditorium lights failed to do much good. I didn't want to bump into any valuable scenery or props. They were messed up enough as it was.

My eyes searched the deepening blackness. The light in the hall between the stage and the orchestra room should have been on. Why would anyone turn it off? I moved forward, believing at any moment the light from the hall would explode into view, lighting the way to the orchestra room like the mouth of a cave leads a miner out of the bowels of the earth into the safe sunshine of the world above.

No light sprang into view. With the trickles of light from the auditorium, I barely made out the opening from the stage to the hallway. Fine. I should be able to see enough in the hall to find a light switch. No sweat.

Sweat. The lights in the auditorium turned off with a clunk I swear I heard. I turned my head, as if I could see anything in the total darkness.

I took a deep breath and stretched out one hand, which held my bow and music folder. My feet slid forward until my hand banged into a wall. Pages of sheet music scattered everywhere. I'd never be able to find them in the dark. What was the wall doing in front of me so soon, anyway? I thought I had a good four or five feet before I reached it. As disoriented as I was, I could easily bump my cello into something and scratch the wood. Or what if I caught my bow on a prop and damaged the horsehair? Cellos are large, expensive instruments, and mine was nice. I couldn't accept even a tiny ding. I felt the wall with my hand and carefully set my cello and bow on the floor next to it. It would be safe until I found a light switch.

Knowing the complexity of stage lighting, I decided my best bet would be to find the light switch in the hall. As I felt my way along the wall, the unmistakable sound of footsteps made me freeze.

"Who's there?" I called. "Do you know how to turn on the lights?"

No one answered. My heart skipped a beat, and I knew. Helping me was the last thing on the mind of that person out there in the blackness. Sure, she knew how to turn on the lights, but she had no intention of doing it. She just turned them off a few seconds earlier. Now she was going to make good on her threat in the note. At least she'd have a hard time finding me in the dark—or she would have if I hadn't called out to her. I wanted to kick myself.

The sound of the psycho's footsteps got louder as she crossed the stage, headed straight for me. I crouched down into a ball and inched closer to the opening to the hall. Okay, shhh. Stop beating so loud, heart. Don't breathe. If I moved and kept silent she'd have a hard time finding me.

I peeked up and gasped as a pinpoint of light shined in my eyes. It was one of the small flashlights stage crew members sometimes use backstage to help them move scenery in the dark. I couldn't see her face, but I knew she saw me.

A gurgling scream bubbled up in my throat as I jumped to my feet and lunged toward the hall doorway. I tumbled through the opening, tripping over my own feet. Two strong arms grabbed me, pinning my bent arms to my chest

My mind spun so fast, I thought I'd drown in the whirlpool of blackness. The footsteps came from the other direction. Who held me now? It was a guy, I could tell. L.J.? Was he helping Marissa carry out the threats she wrote in the notes, or had he written the notes himself?

The thoughts flew through my mind in a fraction of a second, then I realized I had to fight back—no matter who he was. With grunts and screams, I twisted my body and wriggled one arm free. My curved fingers clawed at his upper arm. I positioned my foot to let loose a swift kick to the shin when I heard my name.

"Brittany! Calm down. It's me. It's okay."

"Kyle!" I collapsed into his safe embrace.

"Who's out there?" he asked.

"Someone—someone—" My voice shook, despite my best efforts.

"Stay here." He positioned me against the wall with a gentle shove and, despite my lingering arms around his neck, moved away. Within seconds he flipped the light switch. The hall changed from midnight to noon-day. With determined strides he entered the backstage area. More lights followed. Each new level of brightness slowed my racing heart another notch. A few minutes later he returned carrying my cello, bow and music folder. He found me standing slumped against the wall.

"I didn't find anyone," he said.

My shoulders slouched even more. "You think I'm insane, don't you? I swear, someone was out there."

"I know. I saw the lights go out. I heard someone walk across the stage. Pretty rotten joke if you ask me. When I figure out who did it, I'll break his leg. I'll break both his legs. Here, are you okay?" He extended his hand. Since he held my bow and music folder, he couldn't do much for me. I pushed myself off the wall.

"Thanks," I said, taking my bow and folder

from him. My hand trembled, spinning the tip of my bow in circles.

"You're really shook up," He said as he wrapped an arm around me. I leaned into him. His lips pressed against my hair. I took a deep breath as some of my jitters disappeared.

After we arrived in the orchestra room and set everything on the floor, I slumped into a chair. Kyle pulled another chair in front of me, sat down and placed his hands on my knees.

"You feeling any better?" he asked.

I shrugged one shoulder. "I guess what scares me is thinking what could have happened. I mean, was that person trying to scare me, or were they really going to do something?"

Kyle grimaced. "Don't even think about that."

"I'm glad you were there." I paused. My eyebrows scrunched together. "What were you doing in that dark hall anyway?"

"Waiting for you," he said. "I was going to grab you when you walked through the door, but not like I did. It was supposed to be more like a joke."

He chuckled. "I almost grabbed Mrs. Fleming by mistake. Fortunately, some lights were still on, so I saw it was her. A few seconds later I heard you coming. Then the lights went off. I knew something wasn't right when I heard you call out and the guy didn't answer." He gave my knees a soft squeeze. "It's over now anyway."

"Is it?"

"Well, yeah. Sure. Why wouldn't it be?"

I rubbed my hands up and down my arms. "We can hope," I said, knowing false dreams as I spoke them.

"You'll be okay once you stop thinking about it." His lips turned up in a sly smile. "I know just what you need."

"Oh, do you now?" I said, twitching my eyebrows.

A fake look of shock came over his face. "Get your mind out of the gutter, girl. I had something more civilized in mind."

"Hey, I only meant a kiss."

"We'll get to that later." He rose from his chair, lifted my cello off the floor and leaned it against my knees. With great flare, he presented me my bow.

Ignoring him, I leaned my head against the neck of my cello. "I don't feel like playing."

"That's exactly why you should play." He opened my fingers and pressed the bow into my palm. "Do you need some music?"

"No, because I'm not going to play."

"You're going to play." He moved a music stand in front of me and picked up my folder.

"All right, I'll play. But, only for a minute." I pushed the stand away. "I don't want to do a song from the play."

I positioned my cello between my knees, closed my eyes and let my mind shut down while my fingers took over. I'm not sure which song I played. It was a piece I'd learned in orchestra a year or two ago. I couldn't remember the title, but my fingers had no problem remembering the notes. I let myself sway with the comforting tones and soothing melody.

At the last note, I lifted the bow off the strings, my arm poised in a soft arc. When I opened my eyes, I was almost startled to see Kyle in the room, his gaze fixed on me. He shook his head.

"I love watching you play. The way you move as you make those incredible sounds is like a dance. It's much more graceful than anything we do on stage."

I dropped my bow arm and fingered the strings with the other hand. "It did make me feel better."

He slid his chair closer to mine. "You were playing in the pit the first time I saw you. The way you looked—the way you played—I thought you were the most beautiful thing I'd ever seen. You were so into the music, I don't think you knew a play was being performed along with you. I couldn't keep my eyes off you. Once DeDe yelled at me to get my eyes out of the pit. Do you remember that?"

I smiled and shook my head.

"I watched you enough to figure out you were friends with Amanda. I learned your name from her. Then I came up with that stupid idea to leave a gift under your chair."

"It was sweet."

"Sweet, but corny." He chuckled. "It fit in perfectly with this play. Who sends secret admirer notes in real life?"

I shrugged my shoulders.

"Guys like me who're too chicken to go up and talk to a girl in person, that's who. On the day Amanda brought the lipstick, I was dying to plant a pink smooch right there." He poked the center of my cheek. "I wanted to join that horde of guys who ganged up on you. I thought you wouldn't notice me in the crowd. I didn't even have the guts for that. What I really wanted to do was ask you out, but I didn't have the guts for that either."

"Why not?"

He gave my forehead a soft tap. "Duh—you might have turned me down. You had no idea I was alive."

"I wouldn't have turned you down," I said before I caught myself. "Well, maybe I would have—if I thought you were using me to get to Amanda."

"That girl would have spoiled my plans one way or another. I thought I was doomed when she caught me trying to put the box under your chair. I wished a trap door would open under my feet."

"I'm glad it didn't," I said, reaching for his hand. "For lots of reasons. Right now I'm glad you're here with me."

He leaned over my cello. "I hope I'm always around when you need me."

"I hope so too," I said. In my mind, I kept thinking, *tonight—tonight—tonight...*

Twelve

When Kyle and I walked out of the school, we saw Marissa, L.J. and a bunch of the other pit members on the lawn, chasing around and stuffing dried leaves down each other's shirts. The suspicions I had of L.J. and Marissa in the dark auditorium seemed silly in the bright afternoon sunshine. Everyone looked like they were having so much fun, Kyle and I joined the game. I admit I could have run away from him a little faster, but then he wouldn't have grabbed me around the waist and rolled me into a pile of leaves. I threw a handful into his face.

After we reduced most of the leaves covering the school lawn to microscopic particles, we walked a block-and-a-half to a doughnut shop, each of us adorned with bits of broken leaves in our hair and stuck to our clothes. Kyle, Marissa,

L.J. and I ended up at the same table.

"Do you realize doughnuts are the same shape as onion rings?" Kyle asked. He ripped one in half and both of us took a bite at the same time. He worked his way up the doughnut, but I broke into laughter and backed off before he reached my mouth.

L.J. ripped his doughnut in half and twitched his eyebrows. "Hey, Marissa, wanna try?"

She threw a wadded napkin at him. I wasn't absolutely sure, because of her dark skin, but I'm almost positive she blushed.

L.J. took a bite of his doughnut. He shook the other end at Kyle and, even though he had food in his mouth, said, "You know what, Edmond? We're getting pretty bored in the pit. You need to do something to add a little UMPH to this show."

"Yeah? Like what?"

"That pillow thing you did to Felicia yesterday was great."

"I didn't..."

L.J. spoke on top of his words. "Blowing those

feathers back and forth kept us awake during the second half of the play."

"I liked the lipstick thing," said Marissa, stealing a quick glance at L.J. "You could do that again."

"Naw, it's been done," I said.

"What if I put something different on my lips?" asked Kyle. He hunched his shoulders and twisted his lips into a creepy smile. "Something like in a spy movie—a potion that has no color or taste, but knocks Felicia out for a good twenty minutes."

Stage kisses are full of venom.

I shook my head. Where did that come from?

"We'd stay awake to watch you try to finish the play with a comatose Felicia," said L.J. "No, wait. I think we'd have more fun if she came down in the pit with us. After you knock her out, toss her lifeless body to me."

Marissa frowned and lowered her head.

"You guys are disgusting," I said.

"I've got an even better idea," said Kyle, ignoring me. "You'll want her awake, so, during one of our dance numbers, I'll give her a big spin and fling her into the pit."

Misplaced steps lead to PITfalls.

L.J. growled like a tiger. "Sounds good to me."

"I'm going to the restroom," said Marissa. She pushed back her chair and marched away.

"You know what would be funny?" asked Kyle. "During the final scene, when Inspector Tisdale and I get so mad we grab swords and almost start a fight, you hop up on stage. Hit him over the head with your drumstick. Then you and I will go at it."

"Me with my drumstick and you with a sword?" asked L.J. "I don't think so."

"Okay then, seeing my unfair advantage, you run away. You make various cast members your human shields. Of course, I'll have to kill a few of them to get to you. Then you go behind the sets and start pushing them over on me. In the end everyone will be dead, all the scenery smashed, and you and I will be standing alone in the middle of it."

Prop daggers cut. Falling scenery crushes bones.

"You two better be dead along with everyone else," I said with a splash of acid in my tone.

"Come on," said Kyle, giving me a playful shove. "We're just kidding around."

"I don't think this is the time to be kidding about things like that."

Kyle glanced at his watch. "Yeah, you're right, it's time to head home. I have a bunch of stuff I need to do before tonight's performance."

"That's not what I meant," I said. He didn't seem to hear me.

"Hey, L.J., kick my backpack over here, will you?"

L.J. leaned to the side to look at the pile of backpacks we set on the floor.

"It's the black and gray one," said Kyle. "Wait. Don't really kick it."

"Why? You drama boys carry china dolls around?"

Kyle gave him a disgusted glare. "No. I happen to be carrying some fragile electronic equipment."

"Wires and batteries," said L.J., rubbing his hands together. "Let me at it."

"What is it?" I asked as Kyle unzipped his backpack and pulled out a little black box with a long wire hanging off the side. He held it up for us to see.

"It's a portable mic. I've got some tweaking to do on it at home."

My heart skipped a beat. *A short in the mic is a hair-raising feeling.* Okay. Kyle was hitting too close to home. It freaked me out.

L.J. pushed back from the table. "If you're not going to do any of the tweaking now, I'm gonna to get another doughnut."

I watched him leave before I leaned closer to Kyle.

"Don't they have someone in charge of that kind of stuff?" I asked. "Like Jared."

"This needs my personal attention," said Kyle. "I've got to make sure nothing distracts the audience's attention from me when I'm speaking or singing tonight."

"What are you going to do to it?"

167

"You know, mess around with the wires and stuff. Make sure it's working how I want it to." He returned the mic to his backpack.

"I don't think that's a good idea," I said.

"Why? Are you worried I'll electrocute myself? Well, don't bother. I know what I'm doing. I'll be fine. In fact, I'll be so fine, I'll upstage everyone tonight, even Amanda. Especially Amanda. My dad will be so glued to me, he won't even notice her."

"You're dad?" I asked.

"He's coming tonight, with my mom. He thinks theater's for wimps. I have to show him how hard I work at it and how good I am. I hope." He leaned his elbows on the table and rubbed his temples. "Tonight, tonight, tonight."

I gasped. "What did you say?"

"Nothing. I'm just working myself into a panic. Some of us theater people say, 'tonight, tonight, tonight' when we're dreading opening night, or an evening of homework or something."

"Oh," I said. "Like who?"

"Hmm?" He looked up. "Oh, you know, a

168

bunch of different people." He jumped to his feet. "I've got to get going. My house isn't far from here. I'll walk. I'll see you tonight, Brittany, after I wade through another catastrophe to a triumphant victory."

My eyes popped open. "What catastrophe?"

"You know, the murder, Miss Kline, everything."

"Oh." Was that really what he meant? I held him in place with a hand on his arm. "Kyle, there's something I want to ask you. Amanda and I have both been getting—" I bit my tongue. If I told Kyle about the notes, he'd pretend he didn't know anything about them, and I might lose my advantage of him not knowing my suspicions. I'd be better off waiting and watching until I gathered some evidence. And, you'd better believe, I'd watch him closely.

"You both what?" he asked.

I said the first thing that popped into my mind. "We've both been getting...really...far behind in our homework. So, we thought maybe we'd skip the cast party after the play on Saturday and hit the books. Would you mind?"

His face scrunched up like he'd taken a bite of a lemon. "Of course I'd mind." He leaned over me, his nose almost touching mine. "If Amanda wants to turn herself into a social recluse, that's her problem. As for you," he paused to turn into Edmond while he quoted a line he says to Inspector Tisdale. "I must advise you to abandon her, or you may face the same fate."

He leaned in and kissed me, not noticing my shock over the fact that the line appeared in one of my notes. I closed my eyes and didn't move. A few whoops from some of the pit guys made him stand up. He pulled a piece of leaf out of my hair and flicked it away.

"I better go," he said. "I guess I need to de-leaf myself in the shower."

"Bye." I lowered my eyes to the crumb-covered table and kept them there.

"I'll see you after the show."

I nodded. He left. I picked up an abandoned straw and flipped it back and forth while I tried to reason with myself. Why was I on the verge of convicting Kyle of writing the notes? So he said some things that reminded me of the notes. So what? That didn't prove anything.

I know what Amanda would say. She'd say I was subconsciously sabotaging my relationship with him. She'd probably be right. He simply quoted a line from the play that happened to be in one of the notes. Everyone involved with the production knew that line. I was surprised I hadn't made the connection between the dialogue and some of the phrases in the notes before.

I fished the note that Amanda gave me the previous night from my pants' pocket. Yes, I'd committed a high school fashion faux pas by wearing the same black pants two days in a row. I tried to create two different looks by varying the tops I wore in the morning, before I had to put on my black t-shirt. I spread the note flat on the table.

Prop daggers cut.
Check.

Falling scenery crushes bones.
Check.

Cinched costumes cut off air.
Hmm. Nope, he missed that one.

Misplaced steps lead to PITfalls.
Check.

Stage kisses are full of venom.
Check.

A short in the mic is a hair-raising feeling.
Check and double check. I actually saw him with the weapon.

Jealous cast members wait to pounce.
He didn't specifically get that one either—unless I counted him. Then it was a big check.

Six out of seven. Was I supposed to take that as a coincidence? He also said, "Tonight, tonight, tonight."

"No!" I said, pounding the table with my fist.

The other pit people stared at me. I gave them a weak smile and slipped back into my thoughts.

Kyle didn't do it. He couldn't have done it. He's too nice. As if to prove it to myself, my mind fluttered to the moment in the hall when he stopped to help me pick up the junk that fell out of my locker. He was a decent guy. He—he found the second note among my scattered papers. I hadn't seen it before he found it. Did he find it—or did he plant it?

My heart raced. I found the first and third notes in my music folder. Kyle could have put them there as easy as almost anyone. Maybe something awful had been in the box Amanda caught him trying to put under my chair.

"Calm down. Think this through," I told myself. Why had Amanda and I decided a girl wrote the notes? It was because of the note Amanda received. I remembered my relief when I read the reference to Kyle in the third person.

I flung the straw aside and took a deep breath. That's right. I decided days ago Kyle hadn't written the notes.

The chair across from me banged into the table as L.J. took his seat.

"Marissa isn't back yet?" he asked before shoving the doughnut into his mouth. "Oh, man!"

I looked up at him.

"I thought this was cherry." He turned the doughnut so I could see the apple filling. "I hate apple. If the sign said cherry, wouldn't *you* believe the filling was cherry?"

Before I answered, he sprang to his feet and stomped back to the counter. I chuckled. He had good reason to be mad. I'd believe a doughnut was cherry if the sign said it was. I gulped. I'd believe anything anybody told me. I'd believe Kyle hadn't written the notes if he wrote them in such a way that let me believe he hadn't. If he was capable of everything else associated with this sick game, what was a little deception in one of the notes?

He was more than sick if he was behind this. He was living a total lie and using me to get to Amanda in a more disgusting way than any boy ever had before. Had he concocted this whole

174

plot to throw off Amanda's performance? Was he desperate to look better than her to impress his parents? Or was there more to it?

"You're jumping to conclusions again," I told myself. "Let's assume Kyle is innocent until he's proven guilty." Before the thought completely formed, more evidence elbowed its way to the forefront of my mind. During yesterday's performance, Kyle was the most likely person to slip the jewels out of his jacket pocket. It would have been a piece of cake for him. And, if he hadn't been the one to do it, wouldn't he have noticed they were missing? He had as much opportunity to sabotage the other props as anyone else. Amanda found one of her notes slipped into the pocket of her costume. Who had an easier chance to put it there than the guy who embraced her on stage?

"Circumstantial. All the evidence is circumstantial," I reassured myself. He saved me in the dark hall. He had been there at the exact moment I needed him. Luck? Coincidence? Or had he staged the whole incident to make himself out as a hero in my eyes? What was the point of that?

And he couldn't have done it alone. He would've needed an accomplice. Did that mean we had two psychos to worry about? No. Kyle was genuinely worried about me. His compassion was real. He was a great actor. It was too confusing. I wanted to scream.

Marissa plunked down in the chair next to me.

"Guys are such jerks," she said.

"My thoughts exactly." I jumped to my feet. "I gotta go."

"You can't just leave me here alone!"

"You're not alone; L.J.'s still here."

"But . . ."

"See you tonight." Ignoring her pleas, I slammed through the door and ran back to the school for my car. The drive home was a blur. I pulled into my driveway, switched off the engine and yanked the keys free. Leaving the rest of my belongings in the car, I raced inside, through the entryway and up the stairs.

"Hey, Brittany," Brianna's voice halfway registered in my ears. "Amanda wants you to call her. She said, 'The second you get home.'"

I acknowledged her with a limp wave as I sped to my room. Amanda would have to wait. I had to find something to prove one way or another if I'd just been out with a boyfriend or a demon.

"Where is it," I mumbled as I shuffled through the mess of papers on my desk. I knew I hadn't thrown it away.

"What're you looking for?" Brianna asked from the doorway. "Amanda said the second you get in."

"Mmm-hmm," I murmured. "Ah-ha!"

"What is it?" Brianna sauntered into the room and read the note over my shoulder. "Is this from Kyle? Look! He's asking you for a date."

"It's from yesterday. We already went out." I crumpled the paper into a ball and let it drop to the floor. I laid down on my bed and buried my head in the pillow.

"Don't you want it anymore? You were excited to find it."

"I needed to see something on it, and I did," I said without lifting my head. "Will you go out please? I want to be alone."

177

"Okay," said Brianna as she backed out the door. "Don't forget to call Amanda. She made me promise to have you call her."

"I will," I said. "Close the door behind you."

I didn't want Brianna, or anyone else, to see me, because I stood a good chance of bursting into tears. Great detective that I was, or maybe because I'd seen the play a few too many times, I came up with the brilliant idea of proving Kyle innocent by comparing the handwriting on the notes. A nagging feeling told me they were not the same. When I pulled out the note Kyle left in the box under my chair, I remembered why I never thought the writing was the same. Kyle typed the note to me. He did it so I wouldn't recognize his handwriting from the other notes. Case closed.

Thirteen

Bam! Bam! Bam!

"Brittany! Are you still in there?"

I lifted my groggy head off the pillow to see Brooke peek through the door.

"What are you doing?" she demanded. "Did you fall asleep?"

My brain wasn't functioning.

"I guess," I said. Fighting heavy eyelids, I pushed myself to a sitting position.

Brooke dashed to my bed and pulled me up by the arm. "Do you have any idea what time it is?"

I rubbed one eye with the back of my hand.

"Brittany, the play starts in half an hour!"

"What?!" Her words were a more effective wake-up call than a bucket of cold water in my face. I jumped up and grabbed my black clothes from the closet. "I've got to get changed. I've got to get to the school. I've got to call Amanda!" I dropped the clothes and darted to the hall phone. Brooke followed.

"Mom wants you to eat dinner before you go. It's ready. She sent me to tell you."

"Sure, okay," I said. I punched in Amanda's number. Her mother picked up on the second ring. I groaned silently, wishing a different family member had answered. Mrs. Parker could talk on the phone for hours about nothing, and, with time running against me, I couldn't afford to get stuck with her for more than eight seconds. "I need to talk to Amanda really fast," I said.

"She already left for the school," said Mrs. Parker. "I know she wanted to talk to you before the play tonight, Brittany, but she had to go. She has to arrive earlier than the rest of the cast to get her costumes ready and her hair and make-up done. It's a lot more involved for her than the others because of her leading role. She has so many costume changes for this play. They can be tricky. She'd be in trouble if she didn't have every last dress and accessory laid out right. In fact I was saying to Mr. Elliot the other day…"

"Thanks, Mrs. Parker," I interrupted, even while the politeness software my parents programmed into my brain screamed in protest. "Actually, I need to leave soon. I can't be late for the play either."

"Oh. All right. I should get myself over to the school as well. Our family is attending tonight's performance. We want to make sure we get good seats. I like to sit in the middle of the sixth row. I find it…"

"I really have to go. Good-bye." I hung up before Mrs. Parker said another word. I'm sure I shocked her with my rudeness, but she'd get over it the second she thought about Amanda's big performance.

A glance at my watch made me shriek. I zoomed into my room, tore off my clothes and slipped my long, black dress over my head. Mr. Elliot insisted the pit orchestra dress in formal, concert blacks for the evening performances—which meant black suits for the guys and long, black dresses for the girls—as if anyone in the audience could see us well enough to notice. I didn't have time to put on a slip or pantyhose. My naked feet felt sticky as I crammed them into my black flats. I shoved a brush into my purse as I dashed out my bedroom door.

My dress, which was made of stiff taffeta, crinkled as I flew down the stairs. My mom and I hadn't been able to find a floor-length, black dress in the regular stores—at least not one that was suited for an orchestra performance. We found plenty that made me look ready for a wild night on the town. We'd been forced to make a special order at a bridal shop. I guess it was a bridesmaids dress—the style certainly seemed to be, with poufed sleeves and a big bow in back—but who would choose black as a wedding color? Dracula?

"I'm leaving!" I yelled as I sprinted for the door.

"Not without dinner, you're not."

"I don't have time, Mom."

"Eat," she ordered.

I snatched a forkful of cooked carrots from my plate without bothering to sit down.

Mom nodded. "That's better. We don't want to see you faint before the first act is over."

"You're coming tonight?" I asked through my second mouthful of carrots.

"Dad's coming straight from work and meeting us there," Brianna said with a broad smile. "He wants to check out Kyle too."

Why tonight? I moaned as I chomped down a bite of Mom's grilled chicken. After I shoved in two more forkfuls, I turned to her. "Okay?"

She dismissed me with a nod.

I broke my time record for covering the distance from my house to the school, even though I just set it the previous night when I rushed to save Amanda. She hadn't needed saving then, but I was sure she needed it now.

I screeched to a stop, jumped out of my car and took off across the parking lot. I didn't make a pretty picture, wearing my long black dress and slippery flats while sprinting at top speed. I almost bought it a couple of times when my foot hit loose gravel. At least it was dark and my outfit camouflaged me.

I didn't stop until I reached the classrooms-turned-dressing rooms backstage. I slowed down enough to figure out which was the boys' room and moved on to the girls'. A peek inside showed me flurry of parlor maids and party guests. I squeezed through the door.

"Is Amanda in here?" I asked a passing maid.

She shook her head. "She has her own room, two doors down."

"Thanks." I flung the door open and dashed down the hall, ignoring the girls' shrieks to close the door.

DeDe walked toward me. She paused, her eyes squinting into thin slits over the top of her glasses.

"Why aren't you in the pit?" she asked.

"I'm going there in a minute."

"Hurry."

"I will." Didn't that girl ever relax? She was going to give herself an ulcer before the play closed.

I found Amanda's room and looked inside.

"Amanda!" I crossed the room in four strides

to where she sat having her hair done.

"Brittany! I've been trying to get a hold of you all day. I wanted to talk to you about the..." She glanced at the girl pinning her hair and lowered her voice to a whisper. "You know what."

I leaned close and lowered my voice as well. "What did your note say today?"

"It just said, 'tonight, tonight, tonight.' It freaks me out more than any of the others."

"Mine said the same thing. But, I figured out who wrote them. We won't let him get away with it."

"Him?" Amanda asked, letting her voice rise. "It's a guy?"

I continued to whisper. "It's Kyle."

"No way."

I nodded. "The pieces fit. He's trying to upset you so you won't perform well. He doesn't want you to be better than him."

"That's crazy, Brit. Kyle would never do that. He's a good guy. He's my friend. He's your boy-friend!"

"Not for long."

185

Amanda turned to the girl behind her. "Are you finished yet?"

"Just about," she answered.

"Brittany, you've jumped to the wrong conclusion. You've done it before, you know."

"I know, but things are different this time."

"No, they're not. You're sabotaging your happiness, the same way you do every time you think a guy who likes you likes me."

"I wish you were right, Amanda. But, I know—I KNOW—he did it. You've got to be extra careful around him tonight, on stage and off."

"You sound serious."

"I am. I think I'll find Mr. Elliot and tell him. We can let him decide if he wants to cancel the play."

"No, Brittany. I don't want the play to be canceled. My family's coming to see me tonight."

"Do you want them to watch you get squashed by a piece of scenery? Or cut with one of the prop daggers? He made specific threats about tonight. You can't pretend he didn't."

"Kyle would never hurt me. If he did write

the notes—and I'm still not totally convinced he did—he's just trying to throw off my performance. I'll be fine."

"Done," said the hairstylist. "You've got twelve minutes to curtain." She turned to me and held out her brush. "You want to use this?"

I leaned over and looked in the mirror. Half a dozen pieces of leaf spotted my hair. I snatched the brush and tugged it through the tangled mess on top of my head. Bits of leaf floated to the ground.

"I hope you're right, Amanda," I said. I gave up the battle to save my hair and tossed the brush aside. "I have to go. Promise me you'll watch yourself."

"I will. Go. I'll be fine."

I gave her arm a squeeze before I left. I hoped she was as confident as she sounded.

I decided to make a stop on my way to the orchestra room. I gulped as I knocked at the door of the boys' dressing room—they'd be dressed by now, wouldn't they?

"Come in!" I heard a voice call. Great. Someone

could have at least opened the door and shielded me from anything I shouldn't see. I pushed the door open an inch and peered inside.

"Hey, look who's here," Uncle Conrad yelled as he pulled the door open and exposed me to the roomful of boys. Fortunately, they had finished putting on their costumes.

"It's a witch, come to cast a spell on us," one of the party guests hollered.

"She can cast a spell on me anytime," a butler said. These guys looked like high-class gentlemen, but underneath their costumes they were one-hundred-percent high school boys.

"Is Kyle here?" I asked, knowing the answer. I'd have seen him if he were.

"He probably won't get here for a few more minutes," Uncle Conrad said. He leaned close and gawked at me through his stage monocle. "If you have a good-luck kiss for him, you can give it to me."

I backed out of the doorway.

"Forget it, Drake, she's giving it to me."

"I asked first."

I made a hasty retreat while Uncle Conrad and the party guest battled it out over my non-existent kiss. I was half-relieved I wouldn't get the chance to warn Kyle we were on to him. Wimp that I was, I wanted to delay that confrontation as long as possible. Besides, Amanda would probably take care of it herself. Or would she? She came on stage a lot earlier than he did. I didn't know how much time she had to talk to him between scenes.

Even though I was racing against the clock, I made one more detour before I fetched my cello. It didn't take long to find Jared backstage. He held a long list of last minute details he had to tend to, but he stopped when he saw me.

"Amanda needs you," I said. I could've kicked myself for my choice of words when I saw his eyes light up. I hastened to explain before his hopes rose too high. "She'd kill me if she knew I was talking to you, because she hasn't changed her mind. I have to ask for your help though. Amanda might be in real trouble tonight. The guy who messed up yesterday's performance has been threatening her. He's going to do much worse tonight. Amanda needs protection."

In the course of my speech, Jared's expression changed from exuberant, to despondent, to indifferent and, finally, to gallant.

"Brittany, is there any way Amanda will give me another chance? I know I was stupid..."

I cut him off. "I've got to go. Keep an eye on her tonight."

"You bet," he said.

I glanced at my watch as I jogged to the orchestra room. I couldn't believe it. I had a reasonable amount of time to gather my instrument and head to the pit. I paused mid-stride, my mind a muddle. Did I mention Kyle's name to Jared? I meant to. It'd be easier for him to protect Amanda if he knew who to watch out for. I couldn't remember if I had or not. I debated going back to Jared for half a second, until Mrs. Fleming passed me in the hall.

"Glad to see you're on time, Brittany," she said.

I nodded as I resumed my original course. Jared would manage.

Half the orchestra members sat in their places

in the pit when I arrived. Mrs. Fleming gave me a warm smile.

"Cupid's struck again," Marissa said with a giggle as I scooted past her to my seat. "And I mean he's really struck."

"Huh?" I asked. My music stand answered my question. An arrow stuck out of the book rest, as if Robin Hood and his Merry Men had swept through. I set my music folder on my chair while I examined the arrow. About a mile of masking tape secured it's suction-cup tip to the stand. A note dangled from a piece of string near the blue and red plastic feathers on the other end. I ripped it off and opened the note. It was typewritten. I rolled my eyes before I read it.

You've struck me where it counts, and tonight I hope to do the same to you. After the play, meet me in our spot in the hall where we shared an embrace earlier today.

    Kyle and, Brittany
    Act II, Scene IV, Line 26

"What a romantic," Marissa sighed.

With a twitch of my fingers, I leaned the note toward my chest, out of her range of vision. "You mean what a psychopath."

"Are you going to meet him in the hall?"

"Only if I go armed."

"What do you need to arm yourself with? Mouthwash?"

I shook my head. "Forget it. Hey, do you know what happens in Act II, Scene IV, Line 26?"

"Act II, Scene IV. Let's see, isn't that where Uncle Conrad sings the song about how he's made Felicia his heir and how she'll have to be really responsible? No, that's Act I, Scene IV. Act II, Scene IV is where Felicia and Edmond have sort of fallen in love, but Felicia is cooling it because she's suspicious. Then Edmond corners her and tells her— No, wait. Act II, Scene IV is that dark, scary scene when Felicia discovers her uncle's body. Line 26 must be about the time she realizes someone else is in the room with her—probably, 'Show yourself, or you'll find a dagger through your heart.'"

I felt as if a dagger pierced mine. Kyle would

strike during the scene Marissa described. It suited his needs perfectly. The stage would be scantily lit. He would be able to slither wherever he wanted to go and do whatever it was he planned to do. *Prop daggers cut.* I had to warn Amanda. But, how? And why had Kyle warned me? Nothing that guy did made sense.

My mind churned as I warmed up. I skipped a note when I saw my family in the front row, grinning unabashedly and sitting as tall and proud as if I had won a scholarship to Juilliard. I groaned. Did they have to come tonight? Did they have to witness the disaster about to take place? They'd want to meet Kyle after the play. How would I introduce him? Mom, Dad this is my boyfriend, Kyle. You'll have to excuse him. He's being taken to juvenile court on charges of assault with a prop dagger.

Mrs. Fleming snatched my attention to her with a tap of her baton. I was stuck in the pit until the end of the play. Amanda was going to get hurt, and all I could do was sit and watch.

The curtains rose, and the action began.

Fourteen

I played my cello with a nervous energy that had nothing to do with performance jitters or the tension building on stage within the plot of the play. I was much more worried about the tension building on stage that had nothing to do with the plot.

Amanda entered in Act I, Scene V wearing her violet day dress, the one she wore at the opening of the play—not the fancier crimson evening gown she was supposed to wear. In the next scene, when she wore the correct dress, she turned her back to the audience while waltzing with Kyle at a party. A horizontal slit of white appeared through the dark red of her gown at the waistline. I stole peeks at the stage. As the dance progressed, the white—which I realized was her slip—grew more and more visible.

I imagined the expression on Mrs. Parker's face and the thoughts running through her mind. *I sewed that costume myself. How could the skirt fall off? What have I done?* I'd tell her later it wasn't her fault. I knew the dress had been skillfully made and in perfect condition at one point.

A few of the dancing guests broke character and gawked at the dress. Felicia and Edmond continued to waltz as if the crimson skirt hadn't slipped to the floor—despite Amanda's tugs to keep it up—leaving Felicia in a long, full slip. As she twirled around the dance floor, Amanda slid the skirt offstage with a nonchalant kick.

She was totally calm and in control. Ha. I wanted to laugh out loud so Kyle could hear. His little trick hadn't fazed Amanda one bit. He looked pretty cool, himself. If he was disappointed in his failure, he didn't show it. In fact, he was so much Edmond, finishing the scene as if Amanda were properly clothed, he deserved an Academy Award. I knew he wasn't done for the evening though.

At the end of the waltz, I rested the neck

of my cello against my shoulder and glanced at the audience. Brianna grinned and waved. I was trapped in my seat, but she wasn't. I motioned her to come to me with a twitch of my head. She scrunched her eyebrows and leaned forward an inch. It took another, more pronounced, head twitch to get her to leave her seat.

Crouching low, she stepped forward. She squatted next to me, resting her hands on the pit barrier.

I kept my eyes on Mrs. Fleming while I whispered to Brianna. "I need you to take a message to Amanda."

"Backstage?" she asked.

"Yes." I snatched the pencil off Marissa's music stand, where she always kept one to jot down Mrs. Fleming's instructions, and wrote a quick message on the back of Kyle's latest note.

The costumes aren't the end of it. See other side.

I circled Act II, Scene IV, Line 26 and wrote:

Tonight, tonight, tonight. This is when he's going to do it. Watch him!

I handed the paper to Brianna. "Give this to Amanda. And hurry. There's not much time left."

"Okay." She took the note and moved a crouching step away from the pit. Before she left, she turned back and said, "Kyle is a super hottie." She giggled a bit too loud, causing Brooke to shush her.

I took a deep breath and positioned my cello for the next song. I'd done everything I could. Amanda would have to do the rest.

Brianna returned halfway through the next scene, sooner than I expected.

"I couldn't go backstage," she whispered as she crouched near me again. "Some girl wouldn't let me. I showed her the note, and she said she'd take care of it."

"Who was it?" I asked.

"I don't know. She was nice, but kind of weird. She drinks Tabasco sauce. Yuck! She asked a lot about you and Kyle." Brianna's eyes sparkled in the dim light from my music stand. "Everyone knows what a cute boyfriend you have."

Brianna slid back into her seat before I could prod her for more information. A thousand alarms rang in my head. I couldn't be sure Amanda had been warned. Would she receive the note in time? Who in their right mind drinks Tabasco sauce?

I sat on the edge of my seat during the next few scenes. They passed without any major disasters. Amanda appeared once without a pair of long white gloves and a hat, but only the cast—and Amanda's mother—knew they were missing. Amanda seemed relaxed and confident. I hoped her confidence was due to the fact that she received my message and felt in control of Act II, Scene IV.

The time had come. The curtains opened to a black stage. I shivered as a creepy sensation tickled up my back. Amanda appeared onstage, lighting her way with a single candle. It was battery operated—safety regulations. The effect was realistic from the audience's point of view.

My nerves did a number on me. I wiggled my shoulders to shake off the feeling of a spider crawling into the bottom of my hair. The sensation didn't go away. I raised my hand to the back of my head. It knocked into something thin and hard. I grabbed it as I turned.

Nate, the bass player, gave me an impish grin. I let go of the long bow he used to tickle my hair. I half-glared, half-grinned at him. I couldn't be too mad. He got me, and his joke would have been funny if I hadn't been so tense.

My eyes darted between Mrs. Fleming, in front of me, and Amanda, on stage as she proceeded through the scene. I played the tension-filled background music. Line 26 was coming up fast. My breathing matched the pace of my tremolo.

"Show yourself, or you'll find a dagger through your heart!" Felicia proclaimed. The silent mystery character rushed past her, knocking her candle to the floor as scripted. Amanda screamed. I flubbed a note before I remembered she was supposed to scream. The darkness on stage prevented me from seeing what happened. I heard a lot of scuffling and shrieking, which is what the script called for. After what seemed like ages, the light from an oil lamp—also battery powered—illuminated the stage, revealing Amanda huddled on the floor.

"What happened here?" a deep voice boomed.

"Inspector Tisdale!" Felicia scrambled to her feet and into the fatherly arms of the inspector. "My uncle. Something dreadful has happened. Please, help him!"

Inspector Tisdale pronounced Uncle Conrad dead and discovered the open safe and missing jewels. The scene concluded without a hitch. Even Amanda's costume had been flawless. Kyle must not have had the guts to go through with his plan. Or maybe, because of the warning from me, Amanda had been able to stop him.

Marissa nudged my arm. When I turned my head, she pointed at her music with her bow.

"I was wrong. That wasn't Act II, Scene IV.

It's coming up now."

"What?" I checked her music and then my own, as if it would be any different. Written at the top of the page, where it had gone forgotten, were the act and scene numbers. Clearly II and IV. My stomach did a cartwheel. *Here we go again.*

I barely registered Marissa's whispered, "I'm going to count the lines so we can figure out what Kyle means by Line 26. I'm sure it'll be juicy. This is kind of a love scene."

Edmond and Felicia played the coy games of love. Although, after her uncle's death the previous night, Felicia wasn't quite in the mood and, suspicious of everyone, gave him the cold shoulder.

"Seven," whispered Marissa.

I set down my bow and twisted my fingers together. Thank goodness the cellos didn't have any parts in the background music for this scene. I was free to study the stage for signs of impending doom. I detected nothing. Amanda and Kyle were deep into their roles. Various cast and crew members hovered among the curtains in the wings.

Robert, the butler who brought Felicia and Edmond goblets of wine—it was only grape juice—stood ready and waiting to enter at his cue. Mr. Elliot was the only director I knew who used real food and drinks in his plays. A lot of directors used plastic or invisible food to cut down on messes. Mr. Elliot wanted the real liquid in this scene, to 'preserve the reality of the moment.' Right. Like everything else in the play was so believable.

Wait, where was Robert's tray with the goblets of juice? Oh, there it was. Up near the front of the stage, DeDe stood with the tray. She must have been preparing the drinks, because she poured something into the goblets. I did a double take. She poured something into the goblets!

Stage kisses are full of venom. Felicia and Edmond didn't kiss in this scene, but, if you stretched your imagination far enough, you could say they kissed the goblets with their lips. Venom was like poison. DeDe wouldn't poison them, would she?

"Line thirteen," said Marissa.

I took a deep breath as I pulled on the reins of my galloping thoughts. Okay, so DeDe was Kyle's mystery accomplice. But, they were trying to scare Amanda, not kill her. This was high school, not a daytime soap. DeDe wouldn't put poison in the goblets. I leaned forward to get a better look.

DeDe stood hidden from the audience and the rest of the cast and crew, among the thick curtains on the opposite side of the stage from where I sat. My seat in the pit faced her, and the light from the stage shined enough for me to see her. The bottle she held was small and red. No, it was full of red liquid. The Tabasco sauce! DeDe poured Tabasco sauce into the goblets—into both of the goblets! Did this mean—could it mean? I closed my eyes for a half a second of joyful relief at having Kyle returned to me whole.

How whole would he be after he drank juice laced with hot sauce?

DeDe held the empty bottle over one of the goblets while the last drops plopped into the juice. What would it do to Amanda and Kyle?

They'd certainly gasp and choke and wouldn't be able to speak well enough to finish the scene.

Somebody had to stop DeDe. Didn't anyone see her? I leaned forward as she carried the tray to Robert and nudged him onstage. I twisted in my chair, my mouth opening and closing like a goldfish. This couldn't happen.

Felicia and Edmond each took a goblet from the tray and dismissed the butler with a nod. I rose to my feet as the goblets rose to their lips. The instant before I screamed, half the audience beat me to it. They were as shocked as I was to see Robert stumble back onstage. He bumped hard into Amanda's back, which pushed her into Kyle's front. Goblets fell, and grape juice spilled down her dress and all over the floor. I hoped Mrs. Parker owned a good stain remover. Fortunately, the long-stemmed goblets were made of plastic. The mess wasn't as awful as it could have been.

A hand pulled me down to my seat. "It's okay," Marissa whispered. "They can't drink it now."

"You saw what DeDe did?" I asked.

Marissa nodded. "The two of us probably

have the only seats with a view of where she stood. What a wacko. What's she trying to do? Ruin the play?"

"Or ruin Amanda. Thanks for pulling me back down."

"No sweat. What's the second chair cellist's role, if not to support the first chair cellist?"

I smiled. We let our eyes drift back to the stage to watch Robert scramble to his feet, ad-lib an apology and duck out with a bow. As soon as he walked off, he blew up at Jared, who received his words calmly. A few of the stage crew guys covered Robert's mouth and pulled him farther backstage, where the audience couldn't hear him.

DeDe hustled four parlor maids with wet rags onstage to wipe up the mess. As they worked, I noticed Jared walk up to her in the wings. He showed her the empty bottle of Tabasco sauce. She covered her mouth as if in shock.

My mind calculated like a high-speed computer, sorting and making sense of the facts. Jared found the empty bottle and figured out what happened—although he didn't know DeDe was responsible. He hadn't been in time to keep Robert from going onstage, but, as soon as he came off, Jared gave him a shove. It was the only way he could keep Amanda and Kyle from drinking.

The maids finished the clean up job and scurried out to let Felicia and Edmond finish their dialogue.

I took a huge breath and sank into the back of my chair. Amanda was safe. DeDe wouldn't dare try anything else tonight. More important, Kyle had been cleared for good.

"The juice mess mixed me up, but I think this is it," Marissa whispered.

"Hmmm?" I asked.

"Line 26!"

I snapped to attention, my focus returning to the stage. Edward leaned close to Felicia, gazing with great earnest into her eyes. Kyle broke character for a fraction of a second, something I'd never seen him do before. He glanced into the pit—long enough to lock eyes with me—before he turned back to Felicia to say his line.

"I think about you every second of every day, and I don't want to stop. I can't imagine anything worse than your shutting me out of your life and your heart. Please don't. Let me into your heart—let me in fully."

I'm ready, Kyle. I wanted to shout. *I'm ready!*

Fifteen

The instant Mrs. Fleming cut off the last note of the reprise number, which we played while the cast members took their bows, I laid my cello on the floor and jumped to my feet. I didn't have time to wait for my turn at the stairs. With as much grace as I could manage in my long dress, I stepped on my chair and leaped over the pit barrier.

"You were fabulous, honey," Mom said, her outstretched arms ready for a hug.

"Thanks." I gave her the world's fastest embrace. "Wait here. I'll be right back."

I took the side stairs two at a time and slipped behind the heavy burgundy curtains. The crew scurried about, resetting the props and scenery for the next show. Most of the cast moved toward the dressing rooms, celebrating a fairly successful performance, except Amanda.

She stood center stage chewing out Kyle.

"My family was here tonight," she yelled, jabbing his chest with her finger. "I wanted the show to be good. How dare you…"

"Amanda!" I slid between her and Kyle and held out my arms. "I was wrong. It wasn't Kyle."

The fire in her eyes leapt from him to me. "I knew I shouldn't have trusted you, Brittany."

I felt a soft tug on my hair in the back. Kyle's arm reached around to show me a piece of leaf. He rested his other hand on my shoulder and peered out at Amanda. "What are you guys talking about? What's going on?"

"Haven't you noticed that someone's sabotaging the play?" I asked, stepping aside so the three of us faced each other. "Amanda in particular."

"The crew has messed up a lot. I've been meaning to tell them to get their act together."

"It's not them," I said. "And the attacks on Amanda haven't been mistakes."

"You thought I did it?" Kyle asked me.

Amanda rolled her eyes. "She said she had absolute proof."

"I thought I did."

"Like what?" asked Kyle.

"Well, for one thing, you had that mic at the doughnut shop. I thought you were going to rig it to shock her."

"You're kidding," he said, his eyes bugging out. "I was just trying to make sure it wouldn't cut out on me."

"I should've known. It doesn't matter anymore, though. I know who's responsible for sure this time."

Amanda waved her hands in the air and turned away. "I'm not listening, Brittany. I'm not going to convict another innocent bystander because of your wild theories."

"I saw her with the juice."

"That butler made us spill it," said Kyle. "He ruined the scene."

"It wasn't his fault," I said. "Jared pushed him."

Amanda's head jerked back. "Jared," she said in a whisper. "Jared did this?"

"No. Will you listen?" I asked. "Jared saved

you—both of you. He figured out what I saw, the juice had a ton of Tabasco sauce in it. If you drank it..."

Amanda clutched her neck. "Gag."

"We wouldn't have been able to say our lines," said Kyle.

"Jared had to stop you from drinking it without disrupting the play too much."

"Brittany!" The two of them glared at me.

"What?"

"Who put the Tabasco sauce in the juice?" asked Amanda.

"Watch out!"

We turned. A piece of background scenery, flanked by two heavy pillars, fell toward us. A blur zoomed in and swept Amanda to the side. Kyle and I dove forward as the piece of scenery crashed to the floor. I should have known. *Falling scenery crushes bones.* She told us straight out what she was going to do.

Amanda sat huddled on the floor in Jared's arms. He must have been the blur. She seemed fine, but she could've been hurt—any of us could have. I had to put a stop to this once and for all. I scrambled to my feet and tried to pull Kyle with me.

"My leg's caught," he said. Maybe one of us *had* been hurt.

"Is it broken?" I asked. "Are you okay?"

"It doesn't hurt. It's just stuck."

A bunch of the crew gathered to lift the piece of scenery. I couldn't wait. "You'll be fine. I'll be right back, okay?" Not waiting for his response, I skirted around the scenery to the dark curtain jungle beyond.

The light from the hall to the orchestra room shone bright through the shadowy curtains. She made her escape through there. I raced to the entrance, ready to fight to the death, and slammed into nothing. The hall stood empty—not even a stray pit member was there. Where had DeDe gone? Where would a student director go to distance herself from the scene of the crime? Lines from the play clicked through my mind. She went to create an alibi. I'd find her among the other cast members, directing them in their post-performance duties.

The hall to the dressing rooms was as full as the other hall was empty. Cast members lingered everywhere, in costume and out, in small groups and individually. I saw DeDe right away. She stood, clipboard in hand, next to Robert, engaged in earnest conversation.

I walked toward her, my eyes focused, my pace steady. She knew I was coming. The instant Robert left her side, she looked everywhere except at me.

"DeDe," I said.

She scanned the hallway, a cool, in-control expression painted on her face, as thick and fake as stage make-up. "I'm busy."

"I need to talk to you."

She turned. Her eyes narrowed and her nose crinkled as if she smelled something putrid. "I don't have time to talk to someone from the pit."

A week earlier her comment would have popped my fragile bubble of confidence. Now I let it bounce off me like a rubber ball. I closed the gap between us and stared her straight in the face.

"You have to stop. People almost got hurt. I don't know what kind of game you're playing, but I'm telling you, it's over. Now."

"I'm not sure what you're talking about, Brittany—isn't it?" So much integrity laced DeDe's voice, it might have nicked at my belief in her guilt if I hadn't known better. With her acting abilities, she should have been onstage instead of behind the scenes. When she realized I didn't buy the Shirley Temple routine, she broke character, letting the real DeDe emerge. If I looked close, I knew I'd see a snake's tongue flick between the narrow slit in her lips. "You have no proof whatsoever I've done anything wrong."

I wasn't about to let her intimidate me. "I have my own eyes. I saw you pour Tabasco sauce into the wine goblets."

DeDe cocked her head and raised her eyebrows above the rims of her glasses. "Your word against mine." She pursed her lips while she tapped her pencil against her clipboard. "You know, Brittany, I've noticed some of the pit members haven't given their all to this play. They come late. They stare at the leading man instead of at their music. They can be very disruptive." The overdose of sugar in DeDe's voice made my stomach churn. "I think I'll have a little talk with Mr. Elliot about kicking a certain cellist out of this production."

"That would make you happy, wouldn't it? Having the orchestra fall apart fits right in with your plan to destroy this play. What I don't understand is why you work so hard to make it good, just to turn around and try to ruin it."

DeDe rolled her eyes. "As if it stood a chance of being good. This play is a joke. You know that as well as anyone else involved." She glanced around to make sure no one stood within earshot. "It's the perfect chance for me to test my skills."

I replied by backing off a fraction of an inch, hoping this turned out to be the scene where the criminal spills her guts. I pushed aside the thought that, in every movie I've seen where the criminal spills her guts, she only does it because she's about to kill the person to whom she's spilling.

"I'm a great director," DeDe continued. "It's

my passion. Anyone can direct a corny high school play and have it turn out okay. The real test of a director is being able to put a collapsing play back together, to coax a brilliant performance from cast members who are falling apart. I had to make Amanda fall apart so I could put her back together again. I've done quite nicely, don't you think?"

"You're out of you mind," I said. "If you believe for one second you're going to get away with this, you're crazier than I thought. I'm going to find Mr. Elliot."

DeDe folded her arms across her chest. "As I said before, your word against mine. Who do you think he'll believe? The protégée student director he's worked closely with for hours on end during the last six weeks, or a nobody cellist from the pit?"

My mouth opened, but no words came to fill it. I sensed an increase in traffic in the hall and knew DeDe would soon dissolve into the flow. She leaned close and murmured in my ear.

"Gotta go. I have to prepare for the upcoming

performances, if you know what I mean." She slid her hand across her tight hair and patted her bun. "A great director leaves nothing to chance."

"The great director has forgotten a small detail." I turned to see Marissa arrive to stand by my side. "Every director provides an understudy for the leading roles. I'll bet you didn't realize we have understudies in the pit too."

"What—Who—" DeDe stammered.

Marissa grabbed DeDe's hand and pumped it up and down. "The name's Marissa, second chair cellist. You might say I'm Brittany's understudy. I've studied her ability to observe strange happenings on stage, like the student director hiding in the curtains, pouring Tabasco sauce into the wine glasses."

"You saw no such thing," DeDe said with a trace of a tremor in her voice.

"You better believe I did," said Marissa.

My confidence zoomed through the ceiling. "Shall we go find Mr. Elliot, Marissa? I'm sure he'll be interested in what we—two of us, DeDe—have to tell him. I think he'll also find the pile of notes Amanda and I collected to be fascinating reading. He may order a search of your locker. What will he find, DeDe? Missing props? Scissors used to slash costumes and pillows? Itching powder, mice or bees for the next performance? Do you want to come with us, DeDe? Or would you rather wait for Mr. Elliot to come find you?"

With cocky smiles, the two of us black-clad pit members marched down the hall to make good on our threat, leaving a duly-silenced, soon-to-be-ex-student director slumped against the wall.

I never learned the full extent of DeDe's punishment. The principal worked something out with her parents. If they had asked my advice, I'd have told them to lock her up in a padded room in the house for Demented Directors of Doom.

Part of the punishment was to ban her from drama for the remaining months of her high school career, so the performances on Friday and Saturday went off without a hitch. Marissa and I grinned at each other as we played the strains of the reprise number, while maids, butlers and party guests took their bows. Surprisingly enough, I was sorry to see this play close.

The minor leads stepped forward: Uncle Conrad, Inspector Tisdale and, of course, the real murderer, Miss Kline—Uncle Conrad's personal secretary and Edmond's jealous ex-girlfriend. Life imitates art after all.

When I talked to Kyle after exposing DeDe, he told me I should have shown him the notes earlier. He said he could've figured out she wrote them by reading the script of the play. He reminded me he'd dated her a couple of times before tryouts, but, once he landed the lead and she was appointed student director, he broke up with her. It's his rule, after all. He assured me it was something he planned to do soon anyway. I nodded, understanding why I received notes along with Amanda.

Kyle also told me I should have known he was innocent by listening to his lines in the play. "Felicia, I swear by my love for you, I had nothing to do with your uncle's murder," he said with the grace and style of Edmond. He received a soft punch in the arm and a light kiss on the cheek from me.

Kyle and Amanda entered from opposite sides of the stage and met, clasping hands, in the middle. As the audience rose for a standing ovation, Kyle and Amanda bowed deeply, then stood with their hands high above their heads for a moment before they bowed again.

Amanda did the obligatory acknowledgment of the pit orchestra with a flow of her hand in our direction. The spotlight hit Mrs. Fleming square in the back of the head as the audience clapped. She turned and nodded, arms pounding out the beat. The rest of us couldn't acknowledge the applause because we still played our instruments.

The audience continued to clap. Since this was closing night, Amanda pulled Mr. Elliot onstage to be recognized. She presented him with a bouquet of flowers passed to her by Miss Kline. Kyle darted offstage and returned with another huge bunch of flowers. These would be for the leading lady. I almost fainted when he stepped to the edge of the stage and tossed them to me. I yelped and dropped my bow as the flowers hit my cello. I barely managed to keep them from falling to the ground.

"What a romantic," said Marissa in a gooey voice.

I couldn't play with my arms full of flowers. I blew Kyle a kiss and clapped with the rest of the audience. Jared walked onto the stage and presented Amanda with a bouquet of her own. He whispered to her and pointed to the back of the auditorium. Every head turned. Squeals from girls and whistles from guys bounced over the applause at the huge banner a group of Jared's friends held up, standing on their chairs in the last row of seats. The words, *Forgive me*, jumped from a long sheet of butcher paper in fat, black letters.

I shifted my gaze to the stage. Amanda's face burned red under her pancake foundation. The corners of her mouth lifted into a smile. Did that mean she'd take him back? She wrapped one arm around his neck and, with the whole audience cheering her on, gave him a stage kiss like no other.

I looked into the audience for the faces of my family. Gluttons for punishment, they decided to watch the show a second time. I gave Brooke and Brianna a toothy grin when they waved at me. My family sat next to the Parker's, who—except for Amanda's little brother who slept in his seat—clapped and grinned with as much enthusiasm as if Amanda had given her Broadway debut. Mrs. Parker didn't try to hide the tears dripping down her cheeks. Mr. Parker nonchalantly wiped his tears away when he pretended to clean his glasses. Acting must run in the family.

I gasped out loud when I noticed Kyle's father and mother toward the back of the auditorium. I met them Thursday night, after the commotion died down. They seemed nice enough, but, from what Kyle said, his father wasn't what you'd call a theater fan. Yet, here he was, watching his son for a second time. That must have thrilled Kyle. I couldn't have been happier for him.

When I buried my nose in my flowers to take a deep, heavenly sniff, I noticed a card tucked in the middle of them. I opened it with none of the apprehension I'd experienced with other recent notes. Kyle's handwriting was so sloppy I could barely make out the words. No wonder he typed his notes whenever he could. After much struggle, I realized he'd written,

Please stay for the cast party.

I never got around to telling him the line at the doughnut shop about having too much homework was a lie. I looked up and nodded my answer to him. He smiled and gave me a wink. I nudged Marissa.

"Be sure to stay for the cast party. I'll make sure L.J. stays too."

"L.J.?"

"I've seen the way you two eye each other across the pit when you think no one is looking—and all the flirting that goes on between you. You'd be the perfect couple."

"You think so?"

"I do."

Love was so wonderful, it had to be spread. I now understood why Amanda always tried to fix me up with some guy.

The applause died down. Kyle and Amanda gave the crowd a final wave before they stepped back to allow the curtain to close. The song ended, and Mrs. Fleming congratulated us on being a fine pit orchestra.

We *had* been a great orchestra, but now the play was over. I smiled as I stood up, excited about the things that lay before me. It was time to climb out of the pit.

Acknowledgements

Special thanks to Julie Rader for sharing her knowledge of string instruments. Thanks also to Karlene Browning, Sheila Nielson and Chris Minch for their help, support and friendship.

Kristen Landon lives with her husband and four children in Highland, Utah, surrounded by the beautiful Wasatch Mountains.